LAUREL AND THE LOST TREASURE
by Cassie Kendall

Laurel's pixie friend, Foxglove, pays a surprise visit. He brings exciting news of a hidden treasure. He also brings a request: Will Laurel come with him to find it?

Laurel agrees to help her friend. So they head out to track down the Deeps—a place where the air is said to talk!

Talking air turns out to be just one of the mysteries awaiting them. For the friends find that there's another treasure hunter haunting the Deeps. He's less than happy about sharing his finds with them. Or the surprising story of his past.

Even as his secrets come to light, danger strikes. Laurel is left with a difficult decision. Is she brave enough to face her worst fears in order to save someone else?

STARDUST CLASSICS SERIES

LAUREL

Laurel the Woodfairy

Laurel sets off into the gloomy Great Forest to track a new friend—who may have stolen the woodfairies' most precious possession.

Laurel and the Lost Treasure

In the dangerous Deeps, Laurel and her friends join a secretive dwarf in a hunt for treasure.

Laurel Rescues the Pixies

Laurel tries to save her pixie friends from a forest fire that could destroy their entire village.

ALISSA

Alissa, Princess of Arcadia

A strange old wizard helps Alissa solve a mysterious riddle and save her kingdom.

Alissa and the Castle Ghost

The princess hunts a ghost as she tries to right a long-ago injustice.

Alissa and the Dungeons of Grimrock

Alissa must free her wizard friend, Balin, when he's captured by an evil sorcerer.

KAT

Kat the Time Explorer

Stranded in Victorian England, Kat tries to locate the inventor who can restore her time machine and send her home.

Kat and the Emperor's Gift

In the court of Kublai Khan, Kat comes to the aid of a Mongolian princess who's facing a fearful future.

Kat and the Secrets of the Nile

At an archaeological dig in Egypt of 1892, Kat uncovers a plot to steal historical treasures—and blame an innocent man.

Design and Art Direction by Vernon Thornblad

This book may be purchased in bulk at discounted rates for sales promotions, premiums, fundraising, or educational purposes. For more information, write the Special Sales Department at the address below or call 1-888-809-0608.

Just Pretend, Inc.
Attn: Special Sales Department
One Sundial Avenue, Suite 201
Manchester, NH 03103

Visit us online at www.justpretend.com

LAUREL
and the Lost Treasure

by Cassie Kendall

Illustrations by Joel Spector
Cover Art by Patrick Faricy
Spot Illustrations by Deb Hoeffner

Stardust
CLASSICS

Just Pretend, Inc.
Attn: Publishing Division
One Sundial Avenue, Suite 201
Manchester, NH 03103

Stardust Classics is a registered trademark
of Just Pretend, Inc.

Second Edition
Printed in Hong Kong
04 03 02 01 00 99   10 9 8 7 6 5 4 3 2

Publisher's Cataloging-in-Publication
(Provided by Quality Books, Inc.)

Kendall, Cassie.
    Laurel and the lost treasure / by Cassie Kendall; illustrations by Joel Spector; spot illustrations by Deb Hoeffner. -- 2nd ed.
    p. cm. -- (Stardust classics. Laurel; #2)

    SUMMARY: Laurel the woodfairy and her pixie friend, Foxglove, venture into the Great Forest in search of treasure, and manage to help a disgraced dwarf king in the process.

    Preassigned LCCN: 97-73131
    ISBN: 1-889514-09-8 (hardcover)
    ISBN: 1-889514-10-1 (pbk.)

    1. Fairy tales. 2. Treasure-trove--Juvenile literature. I. Spector, Joel, 1949- II. Hoeffner, Deb. III. Title. IV. Series.

PZ8.K46Lb 1998   [Fic]
                        QBI98-679

Contents

CHAPTER ONE

Company Comes Calling

 must not yawn! I must not yawn!

But Laurel couldn't help it. Her mouth stretched into a huge O.

"Oh, dear!" whispered her good friend Ivy. Then she yawned too.

In moments Laurel's yawn had spread to a whole row of young woodfairies. Someone started to giggle.

At the sound, the Eldest looked up from her reading. Her lips twitched a bit. Then a little more. Finally even she gave way to a yawn.

The Eldest covered her mouth and sat up straighter. "Well, really," she said. "Why are you all so sleepy today?"

Primrose raised her hand. "It was Laurel who started it," she announced.

Laurel sighed. Primrose—proper, perfect Primrose—*never* did anything wrong. But she didn't mind pointing out Laurel's mistakes.

The Eldest turned to Laurel. "Am I boring you?" she asked.

"Oh no!" Laurel exclaimed. "I mean...not really." She fluttered her wings a bit and added softly, "I'm sorry."

The Eldest was teaching a special lesson today. As the oldest woodfairy in the Dappled Woods, she was the keeper of

1

fairy history. Laurel had been sure that any story the Eldest told would be fascinating.

But now Laurel was beginning to wonder. The old fairy had been reading from a journal she had kept many years ago, when she was young. The journal was filled with bits and pieces of fairy life. But it still didn't tell Laurel exactly what she wanted to know about the past.

The Eldest bent over the journal and went on with her reading.

> It's the fifth day of summer. This morning there was a little fog. Today Mistress Fern made a musical instrument. She calls it a harp. She made it from the curved branch of a walnut tree. The strings are thin cattail stems…

Laurel's thoughts soon wandered. She really didn't care how the harp was made. There were so many other things she'd rather know about that day.

A gentle poke brought Laurel back to the present. "I think someone wants to talk to you," Ivy whispered.

Laurel looked where Ivy was pointing. Under a bush, a chipmunk was hopping up and down. He was chattering madly and flicking his striped tail.

"Oh, it's just Chitters," she said. "It's probably nothing important. He's always excited."

"Laurel," interrupted the Eldest. "Is there something you want to say to the class?"

"No, I'm sorry," Laurel said again. But then she continued, "Well, yes. I do have a question."

"Go on," sighed the old fairy.

"I was wondering…What was it like to hear the harp?"

The Eldest's eyes widened. "Why, whatever do you mean?" she asked.

Questions tumbled from Laurel's lips. "What did the harp sound like?" she asked. "How did you feel when you heard it? Did you like it? Or did it sound strange at first?"

"Hmmm...I liked it, I suppose," replied the Eldest. "But really, Laurel—what does this have to do with our lesson?"

"Nothing, I guess," Laurel said quietly.

"Let's turn back to matters that *are* part of our studies," the old fairy suggested.

The Eldest finished her lesson. Then she held her journal in the air and made a little speech. "Please remember this," she said, turning from one young woodfairy to the next. "Your journals are your personal histories. And they are part of the history that's recorded in our book of Chronicles. So take care of your journals. Always tell the truth when you write in them. That's all for today."

Her students rose and said good-bye. Laurel tucked her journal under her arm. She looked toward the edge of the clearing to see if Chitters was still there. But the little chipmunk was gone.

Slowly Laurel walked across the Ancient Clearing, where class had been held. A long time ago, woodfairies had woven together the branches of the trees that surrounded the clearing. Now the trees towered overhead, forming a leafy roof. Even on days like today, when a light rain was falling, the ground below stayed dry.

Laurel reached the far edge of the clearing and stopped for a moment. In front of her stood a hollowed-out tree stump. Behind its polished doors was the book of Chronicles that the Eldest had spoken of. This book was the fairies' most valuable possession, for it held their entire history.

Laurel knew how important the Chronicles were to her

people. And how important their journals were too. So why wasn't I interested in the Eldest's journal? she asked herself.

A quiet voice broke into her thoughts.

"I can see why you started to yawn today," said Ivy. "The idea of making a simple old harp must seem boring after all you've done."

Laurel smiled. It was true that she'd had some interesting adventures. In fact, she was the only fairy in memory who'd left the peaceful Dappled Woods. Those experiences had been exciting—and frightening.

But Laurel shook her head. "It wasn't the idea that seemed boring," she said. "I get goosebumps thinking about what it must have been like to hear that harp."

"Then why weren't you interested?" asked Ivy. "Because I could tell you weren't," she added with a gentle smile.

"I think it's the way the Eldest wrote about it," Laurel said slowly. "She only told about how and when the harp was made. I want to know about feelings and ideas. How did Mistress Fern ever think of such a thing? Did the harp's music sound sad, like winter rain on dead leaves? Or joyful, like birds on a summer morning? Nobody ever writes about such things, so nobody knows!"

"Well, why don't you do it, Laurel?" suggested Ivy. "You can write those kinds of things in your journal."

Laurel thought about that. "Maybe you're right, Ivy," she said. She promised herself she'd do a better job of keeping up her journal. And she'd write more about her feelings. Then young fairies who read her words later would know how she'd felt. If any of them cared, that is.

Laurel smiled. "Why don't you come home with me? I want you to try my new tea recipe. It's made from mint leaves and blueberries."

"I'd love to!" replied Ivy. "Your recipes are always so interesting."

The two fairies made their way along the path. They started out walking. But as the soft rain turned to a steady shower, they took to the air. Like most young woodfairies, they were nearly four and a half feet tall. That meant they actually did more gliding than flying.

They soon reached Thunder Falls, the highest waterfall in the Dappled Woods. Most woodfairies lived far from the falls. They liked quiet spots, deep in the shade of ancient trees.

But Laurel loved the roar and tumble of the waterfall. And the rainbows that rose over the surface of the pond below. So this was where she had built her home, high in the branches of a huge oak. With windows on all sides, the treehouse gave her a wonderful view of the falls.

As the two woodfairies reached the base of the tree, a small shape shot out of the grass. It was Chitters again. The chipmunk was chattering even faster than usual.

"Wait a minute, Chitters!" laughed Laurel. "I can't understand when you talk so fast!"

Before Chitters could say anything

more, another shape darted down the tree trunk. Laurel stared up into a pair of bright, lively eyes.

"Hello, Mistletoe," Laurel greeted her mouse friend.

"Big news!" Mistletoe squeaked back. Her tiny ears flicked back and forth and her whiskers quivered. The clever little mouse looked just as excited as Chitters.

"What's going on?" Laurel asked.

In the same breath, Mistletoe and Chitters delivered their message: "You have company!"

CHAPTER TWO

The Hunt Begins

ompany!" cried Laurel. Visitors didn't often make their way to the Dappled Woods. No wonder Chitters and Mistletoe were so excited.

"Come on, Ivy. Let's see if it's who I think it is!" Laurel spread her wings and fluttered up to her treehouse. The animals dashed up the tree, and Ivy followed.

"Aha!" Laurel cried when she reached her porch.

"Foxglove!" Ivy exclaimed.

Sitting with his feet on the porch railing was Laurel's pixie friend, Foxglove. Mistletoe jumped onto the pixie's shoulder. "He arrived just a while ago!" she said.

"A surprise!" added Chitters. "Unexpected! Out of the blue!"

Foxglove's visits to the Dappled Woods were usually a surprise. The pixies lived miles away in the Great Forest. Few of them had ever set foot in the fairy woods. Even Foxglove didn't visit very often.

The pixie hadn't changed a bit from the first time Laurel met him. He was short and thin—but strong. His shaggy black hair still looked like it hadn't been cut in a long time. Even his cloak and fish-skin tunic looked the same.

"So what have you been doing lately, Foxglove?" asked Ivy.

"Oh, my usual pixie business of scavenging," Foxglove

reported. "Looking for this or that unwanted thing to put to good use." He turned to Laurel. "Talking is thirsty work," he said with a smile. "How about a cup of tea?"

"Why should I serve tea to any old pixie who comes along?" said Laurel. But she was just teasing. Laurel was always happy to see Foxglove.

"Maybe I can trade you something for my tea," said Foxglove.

"A trade?" asked Laurel. "What did you have in mind?"

Foxglove laughed. "How about a curious tale from the Great Forest?"

"Tea coming right up!" Laurel said. While Ivy and Foxglove sat on the porch talking, Laurel went inside. She was soon back with three cups of steaming tea.

Laurel handed out the drinks. As she sat down, the fairy asked, "So what's this curious tale you heard?"

"Well, I've been talking to a lot of animals in the Great Forest," explained Foxglove. "Asking what's what and where's where."

"I still don't know how the two of you talk to animals," said Ivy. She stared at Mistletoe and Chitters, who looked back at her.

Laurel smiled. Sometimes she forgot that Ivy and the other woodfairies didn't know the animals' language. In fact, Foxglove was the only pixie who understood it. Laurel had taught him.

"Mostly it's a matter of listening hard," Laurel said. "And putting up with a lot of chattering," she added with a laugh. Mistletoe and Chitters pretended to be upset at her words.

Laurel turned back to Foxglove. "So what have you heard?" she asked.

"Wonderful stories," Foxglove replied. His voice dropped to a whisper. "Stories of a long-lost treasure hidden in the Great Forest!"

"A treasure!" gasped the others.

"Yes," said Foxglove. "Beautiful jewels and things of silver and gold."

"But whose treasure is it?" Laurel asked.

"I don't know," replied Foxglove. "Right now it doesn't seem to belong to anybody."

"Which means it's free for you to scavenge," said Laurel. "But I thought pixies were only interested in things that were useful. What do you want with jewels and silver and gold?"

Foxglove's eyes took on a strange gleam. "It's treasure, Laurel! Things no pixie has ever brought home before!" he exclaimed. "I'm known as a good scavenger. And I want it to stay that way. So I have to find this treasure before someone else does!"

"But how will you find it?" asked Mistletoe. Laurel smiled. Her bright friend always asked the right questions.

"That's a problem," admitted Foxglove. "I've only heard hints about where it might be hidden."

He glanced at Laurel before going on. "I'm not as good at understanding animals as you are, Laurel. So I was wondering…Well, I was hoping that you'd help me out."

"Absolutely! Positively! No question about it!" declared Chitters. But Laurel, Ivy, and Mistletoe were quiet.

Finally Laurel said, "You mean come with you?" Her heart beat faster. "I'm not sure."

"Why not?" Foxglove asked.

"For one thing, I don't think I'd be much help," Laurel replied. "I have a hard time understanding some animals in the Great Forest. Their language isn't like that of the animals around here."

"Come on, Laurel," Foxglove begged. "It'll be a real adventure."

"I don't know," Laurel said slowly. "I'm not sure a hunt for treasure is worth going out into the Great Forest." She couldn't help thinking about how scary it sometimes was out there.

"Don't forget the trolls," added Ivy with a shudder. She had heard Laurel's stories about the evil creatures who lived in the bog at the forest's edge.

"Believe me, I haven't forgotten," said Laurel. She turned to Foxglove. "You'll go even if I don't, won't you?" she asked.

The gleam in Foxglove's eyes deepened. "I have to," he said. "This is the chance of a lifetime! Why, I bet we'll end up with sacks and sacks of treasure. Rubies and diamonds and emeralds. Long gold necklaces. Thick silver bracelets…" He trailed off as the dream swept over him.

Laurel stared out at the peaceful woods below her. Yes, she was still a little scared of the Great Forest. It was a much wilder world out there. Not calm and gentle and safe like the Dappled Woods.

But Laurel was also a little scared about Foxglove's hunger for this treasure. The pixie was much too caught up in the whole idea. He didn't seem to be thinking things through. Foxglove might be a great scavenger, but he needed someone else along. And as his friend, Laurel knew she was that someone.

She nodded. "All right, I'll come."

"If Laurel's going, I am too," said Mistletoe bravely. Laurel gave the mouse a smile of thanks.

Foxglove clapped his hands and turned to Ivy. "What

about you? Would you like to come?"

"Me?" gulped Ivy. "Oh no, Foxglove. I'm not like Laurel. I'll probably never be brave enough to go outside the Dappled Woods. And that's fine with me! Why, the very idea makes my stomach go all funny."

Then Ivy frowned. "I'm not so sure that you should be going either. Stories of treasure don't mean there really is one."

"Ah, but I have more than stories!" said Foxglove with satisfaction. He reached into the scavenging bag that he always carried. "Look at this!"

He pulled out a chain of fine gold. Each link caught and held the light.

"It's lovely," said Laurel as Foxglove handed her the chain.

"It *is* lovely," said Ivy. "Where did you get it?"

"From a badger I met," Foxglove said. "I traded him something for it." The pixie's eyes danced merrily.

"Well, where did the badger get it?" asked Mistletoe with a twitch of her whiskers.

"I don't know," admitted Foxglove. "He wouldn't tell me. And I didn't want to make him mad. You know how mean badgers can be."

"Absolutely!" agreed Chitters.

"But this shows that there really is a treasure," said Foxglove. He took the chain back and dropped it into his bag.

"All right," Ivy said. "Just promise me that you'll all be very careful." She gave Laurel a big hug. "At least this treasure hunt will give you something to write about in your journal. And don't forget to tell how you feel about things."

"I won't," promised Laurel.

Ivy said good-bye and headed down the ladder of the tree-house. Then Laurel went inside to pack her traveling bag.

After having gone on several adventures, Laurel knew what she'd need. Some food, a soft blanket, and extra clothes for a start. Remembering how dark the Great Forest could get, she added two candles. Finally she packed her journal and a pencil. She was done!

Before leaving, Laurel took a long look around her house. Even on a rainy day like this, her home seemed so warm. Colorful rocks, shells, and feathers filled every shelf. Bright woven rugs covered the floor. And a pretty quilt she'd started making lay at the foot of her canopied bed. It all looked beautiful—perhaps even more so because she was going away.

Laurel smiled. Well, everything would still be waiting for her when she got back. She picked up her bag and went out to join Foxglove and her animal friends.

"I'm ready," she announced.

As she reached the bottom of her tree, Laurel noticed that the rain had stopped. But clouds still hid the sun. It looked like the rain would continue for days. And there were signs that a thunderstorm was on its way.

Unlike most woodfairies, Laurel loved thunderstorms. But that was when she was safe in her comfortable home. She hoped she'd be back before the worst of the storms hit the Great Forest.

The four travelers set off. In about an hour's time, they reached the edge of the Dappled Woods. The tame, neat land of the fairies gave way to the gloomy Great Forest. Here the trees grew close together. Thick vines made their way down tree trunks and snaked across the trail.

Laurel followed Foxglove into the wild woods. "Do you know where we're headed?" she asked.

"Not exactly," said Foxglove. "But from what I've heard, this is the path we take. I thought we'd get more directions from the animals we meet along the way."

Laurel listened carefully as they walked along the trail. The calls of unfamiliar birds and animals filled the air. Strange rustles came from the underbrush. Far overhead, something moved through the trees.

Laurel shivered a little. It was such a dark, mysterious world. But that's what makes this an adventure, she thought. And she was glad that Foxglove wasn't going off alone.

Laurel began to look around. She may as well enjoy being out in the forest again—even with all its unknowns.

Then Laurel smelled something. Something awful!

She turned to her friends. "That smell!" she exclaimed. "It's horrible! What on earth—"

Laurel's voice caught in her throat. Suddenly she had a terrible feeling that she knew what the horrible smell was.

"Trolls!" she whispered.

CHAPTER THREE

News and Clues

rolls! There was nothing more frightening! The big, ugly creatures were enemies of all the good creatures in the Great Forest.

Foxglove looked around wildly. "Hide!" he shouted as he dashed into the underbrush.

Mistletoe and Chitters followed him. But Laurel remained standing in plain sight. Turning to look for trolls, she'd spotted a black-and-white animal on the trail.

Now she called out a warning. "Hurry up! You'd better hide too."

With his tail raised in the air, the animal jabbered something to her.

Laurel listened carefully. He didn't seem to be talking about trolls. But he did seem to be saying something over and over.

Then Laurel caught the animal's words. "Sorry! Sorry! Sorry!" he was crying.

What is he so sorry about? thought Laurel. Well, they'd have to settle that later. Right now, the important thing was to get everyone into hiding. She started to hurry down the path toward the animal.

Just then Foxglove stuck his head out of the underbrush. He spotted the animal too. "So that's it!" he exclaimed. Then he saw where Laurel was heading. "Laurel! No!" he cried.

"Don't go any closer to him!"

The pixie crawled out from under a bush. "Come this way!" he called. With one hand over his nose, he quickly headed up the trail.

Laurel shrugged and followed Foxglove. After all, he knew the forest much better than she did. And sure enough, with each step down the trail, the smell became less noticeable. Finally the air seemed clear.

Laurel turned back to see what had become of the creature. He was right behind them—still jabbering away.

"What are you talking about? Why are you so sorry?" she asked the animal.

"Laurel," said Foxglove. "He's a skunk!"

"Oh," said Laurel weakly. So that was the smell! She'd heard about skunks. She knew they could spray a horrible scent when they were frightened. But this was the first time she'd actually met—or smelled—one.

"Sorry! So sorry!" the skunk said again. "You scared me. You shouldn't go marching through the forest like that!"

There was a rustle nearby. The skunk whirled and raised his tail.

"Stop!" cried Laurel. "It's all right! It's just our friends."

Mistletoe and Chitters popped out from the bushes and ran to Laurel's feet. Slowly the skunk lowered his tail.

"You seem a little nervous," Foxglove said.

"Well, maybe," muttered the skunk. "It's a nervous world, you know. One can't be too careful."

Then he looked at Laurel. "What are you doing here?" he asked. "I've seen plenty of pixies. But you're a woodfairy. You're not supposed to be out here, are you?"

Laurel was surprised. Did everyone know that fairies

never left the Dappled Woods? "Well, I'm a bit different from most woodfairies," she said.

"I guess so," said the skunk. "So what are you doing?"

"Looking for treasure," answered Foxglove.

That made the skunk sit up and pay close attention. "Treasure?" he said. "More talk of treasure?"

"*More* talk?" repeated Foxglove.

"What have you heard?" asked Laurel.

"I've heard stories," said the skunk. "And that's not all. Just the other day, a raven was showing me some sparkly things."

Foxglove leaned forward. He breathlessly asked, "Was it treasure?"

"That's what she called it," replied the skunk. "But you can decide for yourself. She dropped a piece as she flew away."

"Where is it?" Foxglove asked. "Can I see it?"

"Come this way," replied the skunk. He turned and headed off the trail.

Foxglove took off after the skunk, his fingers twitching restlessly. Laurel looked at her animal friends and shook her head. "He's got nothing but treasure on his mind," she sighed. "We'd better keep an eye on him."

The skunk led them through the thick bushes to a huge elm tree. "I think the raven dropped it around here." He began to nose about in the dirt.

Soon the animal drew back, pulling something out of a small hole. "There!" he said with satisfaction. "What did I tell you?"

"Is it all right if I touch it?" asked Foxglove.

17

"You can have it," answered the skunk. "I don't want it."

Foxglove's hand darted forward and he snatched the object. Holding his breath, he studied it for a moment. With a delighted smile, he held up the bright red jewel.

"It *is* treasure!" exclaimed the pixie. Then he looked at the skunk. "And you say I can have it?"

The skunk wiggled his tail, and Mistletoe backed away. "Take it," he said. "It's my way of saying I'm sorry for almost spraying you."

"Thanks," said Foxglove. But he wasn't looking at the skunk. His eyes were on the flashing jewel in his hand. "We have to talk to this raven!" he said in a low voice.

"Do you know where we can find her?" Laurel asked the skunk.

"Ravens come, and ravens go," replied the animal. "I don't know where this one is now. But she told me she found her sparklies in New Warren, where the rabbits live."

"I've never heard of rabbits having treasure," said Mistletoe.

"You've never heard of skunks having treasure either, have you?" asked Foxglove with a laugh. He dropped the jewel into his bag.

Laurel gave her friend a worried look. She'd never seen him act this way. Like all pixies, Foxglove loved to scavenge. And on their adventures together, he usually looked for things to take home. But the adventure itself had always seemed more important to him than the scavenging. Until now.

Yet Laurel too wanted to know more about this treasure. There must be a wonderful story behind it! And if only Foxglove were acting like his old self, he'd be interested in the story as well.

Laurel smiled at the skunk. "It was nice meeting you," she said. "And thanks for your help."

"You're most welcome," said the skunk. "And I *am* sorry about the smell." He nodded good-bye and headed off, his tail still flicking.

Foxglove turned to Laurel. "Let's go and talk to the rabbits!"

"Well, I agree with Mistletoe," said Laurel. "There's not much chance of rabbits having a treasure. But we'll go anyway."

So the four friends made their way back to the trail. By the time they reached New Warren, the clouds had parted. The sun shone down on a flower-filled meadow. Dozens of rabbits were sunning themselves there. But when Laurel and her friends came close, the rabbits shot into their holes.

A minute later, curiosity got the better of them. Twitchy noses began to poke up through the grass.

Finally a small gray rabbit hopped up to the visitors. "Hello," she said. "Who are you? What are you doing? Why are you here? What do you want?"

Laurel laughed at all the questions. She had no trouble understanding this little creature. Rabbits often made their way to the Dappled Woods. She'd talked with them many times before.

"My name is Laurel," she said. "And these are my friends. We wanted to ask *you* some questions."

By now several other rabbits had come forward. "Questions?" said one. "What questions?"

"And why ask us?" said another.

"We're looking for a lost treasure," replied Foxglove. "We heard that some sparkly things were found here."

"That's right," said the gray rabbit. "In the stream. I'll show you!" She hopped off toward the far edge of the meadow.

Laurel and her friends followed the rabbit. And a whole line of curious rabbits followed them. Soon they all reached a bubbling stream.

"Look in here," said the little rabbit. "Sometimes there's treasure. And sometimes there's not."

Foxglove peered into the stream. Then he splashed in and began wading through the water. Laurel noticed that he wasn't being very careful. He kept slipping and sliding over rocks and branches.

Laurel turned back to the rabbits. "Do you know where the treasure comes from?" she asked.

"Maybe birds drop it," said one rabbit.

"Or it floats here," suggested another.

"Or it falls out of the trees," said a third.

"Hmmm," said Laurel. "Well, thanks for answering my questions."

The rabbits hopped off. Soon they had forgotten all about their visitors.

"Silly animals," sniffed Mistletoe. "They didn't tell us anything important."

Just then a shout came from upstream. "Come and look!" Foxglove yelled.

The three friends ran along the bank toward Foxglove. The pixie was standing in the middle of the stream. Water dripped from his clothing, but he didn't seem to mind. In his hand, he held another golden chain. This one was even longer than the first.

"More treasure!" he cried. He started toward them. But his eyes were on the chain instead of where he was going.

"Be careful!" warned Laurel.

Too late! Foxglove slipped. There was a tremendous

splash, and the pixie landed in water up to his neck.

Laurel couldn't help but laugh at the sight. She waded into the stream and helped Foxglove to his feet.

Soon they were both back on dry land. Foxglove hardly seemed to notice. He was busy studying his latest piece of treasure.

"Foxglove," said Laurel. The pixie didn't even look up.

"Foxglove!" she said again, this time in a loud voice. Her friend finally raised his eyes.

"If you're still interested in this treasure—" Laurel began.

"*If!*" yelped Foxglove.

"Then we should head upstream," Laurel continued. "I think the water carries things here. Just like the stream at Thunder Falls. It brings lots of things along with it. They all end up at the bottom of the pool near my treehouse."

"So if we follow the stream, we'll find the treasure," said Foxglove.

He added the chain to his bag. "Let's go!" He set off at once.

For the rest of the day, the little band walked beside the stream. It led them steadily uphill. With every passing hour, the stream got narrower. And the going got harder.

"Do you think it's much farther?" panted Foxglove when they stopped for a rest. "Treasure hunting is a lot of work!"

"You've always said it's hard to be a great scavenger," laughed Laurel. "And I guess you're right. I think we may need to go all the way into the mountains."

Ahead of them, they could see cloud-covered peaks. The mountains were huge—much taller than the tallest hills in the Dappled Woods.

"Well, we'd better keep moving," said Foxglove.

"I'm ready," said Laurel. "Oh, Foxglove, I've always wanted

to see the mountains up close. They're beautiful."

"I hope you still think so later," said the pixie. "After we've been climbing for a while."

They set off once more. Sometimes Laurel led the way, and sometimes Foxglove did. Slowly the rain clouds gathered again, and the sky grew darker.

Finally Laurel, who was in the lead, paused. "I wonder if we should stop for the night," she said. "It's getting—"

"Ooof!" cried Foxglove.

Laurel turned. The pixie was flat on the ground. A large, snarling creature had him pinned down. Chitters and Mistletoe had disappeared into the bushes.

Laurel didn't even stop to think. "Get off!" she shouted. She swung her traveling bag over her head. As hard as she could, she smacked it down on the creature's nose.

"Ow!" cried the animal. At once he leapt off Foxglove and flattened himself in the dirt. With both paws over his nose, the animal groaned softly.

Laurel helped Foxglove to his feet. Then she turned back to frown at the creature. "Why did you attack him like that?" she asked angrily.

The animal slowly lifted his head. "I'm a bobcat," he sniffed. "That's what I'm supposed to do! At least that's what my mother taught me. She didn't say anything about *being* attacked." He sniffed again.

"Well, we won't hurt you if you don't hurt us," Laurel promised him.

The bobcat sat up. He stared nervously at Laurel. And Foxglove stared nervously at the bobcat.

"Agreed," the bobcat finally said. "Anyway, what are you doing here?" he asked. "Woodfairies don't belong out in the

Great Forest. I'm not the only dangerous beast out here, you know." He showed his sharp teeth, and Foxglove backed away.

"Oh, stop it," said Laurel.

The bobcat gave a playful flick of his tail. "Can I help it if the pixie doesn't like my smile?" Then he continued, "But back to my question. What are you doing here?"

"We're looking for a lost treasure," said Laurel.

"Lost treasure?" repeated the bobcat. "Why?"

"Because we want to know all about it," said Laurel. "Because it's interesting. And there's sure to be a great story behind it," she added. "Like who hid it? Why? And how—"

"And because it's treasure," interrupted Foxglove. "Have you heard anything about it?"

"I've heard tales," the bobcat answered slowly.

Foxglove lost his fear. He bent down until he was nose to nose with the bobcat. "Exactly what have you heard?" he asked.

The bobcat licked his lips and curled his clawed toes. Foxglove didn't seem to notice. But Laurel picked up her traveling bag, ready to use it if need be. The bobcat gave the bag a sidelong glance and drew back.

"I've heard there's a treasure lost in the Deeps," he growled.

"The Deeps?" said Foxglove. "Where is that? And what is it?"

"I'm not sure," said the bobcat. "I think it's high up in the mountains. A place where the air talks. That's what I know."

"The air talks?" said Laurel. "How can the air talk?"

"That's what I *don't* know," said the bobcat. "And I don't care to find out."

Then the bobcat turned and melted into the forest.

Laurel and Foxglove stared after him. "I wonder what he meant," Foxglove said.

"I'm not sure," said Laurel. "I'll think about it later. After we're camped somewhere for the night."

Mistletoe and Chitters came out of their hiding places. The four friends started along the trail again. Soon they found a good spot and settled down.

"I'm really tired," said Laurel. She handed Foxglove some bread from her bag.

"I'm not," said Foxglove. In spite of his words, he leaned back against a tree trunk.

As the sun set, the sky became clearer. Laurel drank in the beauty of the night. "This is a real adventure, isn't it?" she said after a while.

There was no answer. Everyone else was asleep—even Foxglove.

Then Laurel remembered her promise to Ivy. She took her journal and pencil out of her traveling bag and started to write.

At last Laurel finished telling about her day. Carefully she repacked her bag and pulled up her blanket.

Just as she was about to close her eyes, something blocked out the moonlight. A rushing sound filled the air as hundreds of dark, winged creatures flew overhead.

"It's unusual for birds to be flying around at this time of the night. I wonder what kind they are?" Laurel asked herself.

As she drifted to sleep, she caught a whisper from the creatures. Over and over, they said the same word:

"Treasure…treasure…treasure."

CHAPTER FOUR

Over the Edge!

he soft sound of rain on the leaves woke Laurel. She lay there for a moment, trying to remember something. Something important. What was it?

Suddenly it came back to her. The word she'd heard the birds whisper over and over. "Treasure!"

Laurel sat up. She wondered whether she should say anything to Foxglove about the whispers. He was really much too interested in finding this treasure.

But she knew she had to tell him. Foxglove wasn't going to give up his hunt. And she had to admit that she was curious about the treasure too.

Laurel reached over and shook the sleeping pixie. "Wake up, Foxglove! I have to tell you something!"

Foxglove groaned and opened one eye. Then he opened the other. "What is it?" he asked sleepily.

"Last night I saw something strange," Laurel said. She told him about the creatures that had flown overhead.

"Bats," announced Foxglove. He yawned. "Bats fly at night. There's nothing odd about that. Not out here."

He pulled his cloak around him and closed his eyes again.

But Laurel wasn't done. "Foxglove! They were whispering the word 'treasure.' Now *that's* strange, don't you think?"

At last Foxglove was awake. "They said 'treasure'? What

else did they say?"

"That's all I could understand," answered Laurel.

Foxglove scratched his head and thought for a while. "Maybe this is another clue to where the treasure is hidden."

"What do you mean?" Laurel asked.

"We're trying to figure out just where this place called the Deeps might be. Well, bats live in caves. Caves can be deep. And the mountains are full of caves."

Laurel broke in. "So the Deeps must be a..."

Her voice dropped off suddenly. Her face turned white.

"Laurel, what's wrong?" asked Foxglove.

"We have to stop hunting for this treasure," Laurel said.

"What are you talking about?" asked Foxglove. "We're getting close! We can't give up now!"

"We can if it means going into a cave!" Laurel whispered. "Caves are dangerous!"

Foxglove looked at her in surprise. "You're afraid of caves? I didn't think anything frightened you very much!"

"I don't like places that are dark and closed in," replied Laurel. "I can't imagine going into a cave. And I don't want you going into one either."

"Well, I'm not scared!" said Foxglove. "If the treasure's hidden in a cave, that's where I'll be looking!"

"Foxglove!" cried Laurel.

But the pixie paid no attention. He scrambled to his feet. "Where have Mistletoe and Chitters gone?" he asked. He called their names, and soon the two came racing up.

"The rain is ending," reported Mistletoe.

Chitters gave his wet fur a shake. "It's about time!"

"We have to get started," said Foxglove. "But we'd better eat a good breakfast first. The climb will be harder today."

After eating, the four started off. It wasn't long before they knew that Foxglove had been right. Trees leaned over the path, forcing them to duck under the branches. In places huge rocks and logs blocked their way. And all the while, the mountains towered overhead.

On and on they climbed. After a time, the stream became even narrower and its banks steeper. The path led uphill, away from the water. For a time, they could see the stream from the trail. But then it disappeared from sight.

The band of explorers stood on the path and looked down at the rocks. "What do we do now?" asked Laurel.

"We can't follow the stream anymore," sighed Foxglove. "But I think it must begin somewhere up in the mountains. Let's stay on the trail and see if we can find it again when we get higher." He turned and started up the path.

The friends had to stop every few hours to rest. Whether resting or climbing, they saw no sign of a cave—or a treasure. Late in the afternoon, they stopped again. They sat for a while, looking at the winding trail that lay ahead.

"I had no idea how hard it was to climb a mountain," Laurel sighed. "And we aren't even on a very high one. But the climb is worth it. You can see so much from here!"

"It is beautiful, isn't it?" said Foxglove.

"Too rocky!" complained Chitters. "Too much work."

"Mistletoe doesn't seem to be having any problems," said Laurel. Then she glanced around. "Why, where *is* Mistletoe?"

"She was right ahead of me a few minutes ago," replied Foxglove. He stood up and checked the path.

"She must not have realized that we stopped," said Laurel. "I hope she's not lost!"

Foxglove climbed to the top of a rock. But after looking in every direction, he still couldn't spot the little mouse.

"Mistletoe!" he called. "Mistletoe, where are you?"

The only answer was the echo of his own voice.

"Let's see if she's farther ahead," said Laurel.

Quickly the three started to search. Laurel looked along one side of the trail. Foxglove looked along the other. And Chitters ran through the bushes that grew on the nearby slope. Again and again, they shouted Mistletoe's name. Again and again, there was no reply.

Finally Chitters called from above. "She came this way," he trilled. "Follow me!" The chipmunk took off. Laurel and Foxglove scrambled up the steep hill after him.

"Hurry! Hurry! Hurry!" chattered the chipmunk. Laurel and Foxglove tried to keep up, but they soon lost sight of him. They had only his excited voice to follow.

Suddenly Chitters cried, "Watch out!"

The warning came too late. The ground under Laurel's feet disappeared. Ahead of her was only empty space!

Laurel gasped and fluttered her wings wildly. But then Foxglove crashed into her and she began to fall.

In terror, Laurel reached out to grab a tree branch. Chitters was already clinging there, chattering in fear.

But the ground was slick from the rain. Laurel's feet slipped. And then all three of them started to fall over the edge of the cliff!

CHAPTER FIVE

The Air Talks

aurel screamed as the tree bent and swayed. But not a sound came from Foxglove. He was too scared. As for Chitters, he held on with all his might.

The tree bent farther and farther over the cliff. For what seemed like forever, the three friends swung in the air. But the branch held.

Slowly Laurel got her feet back onto solid ground. She and Foxglove untangled themselves and crawled back from the edge. Then the pixie reached out and grabbed Chitters from the branch.

As they all struggled to catch their breath, they heard a squeak below. "I'm here!"

"Mistletoe!" cried Laurel. She got down on her stomach and crept to the edge of the cliff.

Laurel's head spun. Far below was a small green valley. Sharp rocks and huge trees surrounded it. A stream flowed across the valley and disappeared into the rocks at the base of the cliff. It had to be the same stream they'd been following.

"Mistletoe!" Laurel called again.

There was a scrambling sound nearby. Mistletoe's head popped into sight.

"I found something!" the mouse announced. "Come

here and look!"

"We can't," objected Laurel. "It's much too steep!"

"It's steep, but you can do it," said Mistletoe. "I was going so fast that I fell over the edge. But I landed on a narrow trail. Just follow me." With that, the mouse disappeared again.

Chitters shook himself. "Scary! Frightening! Horrible!" he muttered. But he followed his friend down the cliff.

Laurel looked at Foxglove. The pixie was pale. She knew how much he hated high places. He didn't even really like going up into her treehouse. However, she could tell that he was getting ready to start down anyway.

"Do you want me to go first?" asked Laurel.

Foxglove straightened his shoulders. "You don't have to," he said bravely. "But you can if you want," he added with a weak smile.

So Laurel moved closer to the edge. Mistletoe was right. There was a path—of sorts. It twisted back and forth before finally reaching the bottom of the cliff.

"I see the trail, Foxglove," Laurel said. "And there are lots of trees to hold on to. We'll be fine."

Laurel started down, with Foxglove close behind her. The hill was muddy and covered with wet leaves. Once, Laurel had to flap her wings to keep from tumbling off the trail. Foxglove sat and slid down that part.

At last they reached the bottom. As Laurel stopped to rest, she looked around in wonder. The valley was even more beautiful than it had looked from above. Leaves rustled in the soft breeze, and a carpet of thick grass covered the ground.

Mistletoe and Chitters darted through the grass. "Hurry! Please do! Yes, hurry!" cried Chitters.

The animals took off toward a grove of trees. Laurel and

Foxglove followed. Parting the branches, they stepped into a quiet glade.

"Oh, it's lovely," breathed Laurel.

The glade was bordered on all sides by rocks and trees.  The sun had finally broken free of the clouds. Now light poured into the glade and sparkled on the stream. And here and there, bright flowers added splashes of color.

"Yes! And look at this!" said Mistletoe. She ran to a huge oak tree that grew at the edge of the glade. There stood a rough table and bench made from thick stumps. Nearby were a wooden chair, an old backpack, and a rolled-up blanket.

"It looks like somebody is living here," said Laurel.

"I think you're right," agreed Foxglove. "But who would live way out here? Unless…"

Foxglove held his scavenging bag tightly against his side. "Unless someone else is looking for the treasure," he whispered. His eyes darted in all directions.

"Well, let's find out who's here," said Laurel. Stepping into the middle of the glade, she cupped her hands around her mouth. "Hello! Is anybody here?" she called.

Silence.

"Hello!" Laurel called again.

This time a deep, angry voice boomed back. "Leave this place at once!"

The four friends spun around to see who was talking.

"Who's there?" Laurel asked.

"And where are you?" yelled Foxglove.

"Leave!" replied the voice. "Leave while you can!"

The voice was everywhere. It came at them from all sides. But there was no one else in the glade!

"We've found it!" cried Foxglove. "We've found the Deeps! The air is talking! Just like the bobcat said it did!"

"Foxglove, you know the air can't talk," said Laurel. "There's someone here."

"I suppose you're right," admitted Foxglove. He shouted, "Why do you want us to leave?"

"We don't mean you any harm," added Laurel. "We just want to talk to you."

"Well, I don't want to talk to you!" roared the voice.

"Rude, rude, rude!" complained Chitters.

"Shhh!" said Laurel. "I'm trying to figure out where his voice is coming from."

"Maybe we should just go," said Mistletoe.

"I'm not leaving," Foxglove stated firmly. "Not now."

To his surprise, Laurel agreed. "We have to stay," she said. "Just listen to that voice."

She called out again, "Why won't you talk to us?"

"I don't want to!" The sound echoed all around.

"I see what you mean," said Foxglove. "He sounds old and kind of shaky."

"Do you need help?" shouted Laurel.

"Help! Certainly not! I just need to be left—"

A crash cut off the voice. The crash was followed by a thud. Then, instead of a roar, they heard a groan of pain.

Unwelcome Guests

hat happened?" cried Laurel. "Are you all right?"
The only answer was another groan.

"He's hurt!" she said to Foxglove. "We have to find him and help!"

"I'll check over here," said the pixie, heading for a big rock. Meanwhile, Laurel ran to the other side of the glade.

"We'll search too," said Mistletoe. She and Chitters raced into the nearby forest.

After a few minutes, Foxglove reappeared. "I think I found him!" he called. "Follow me!" The pixie ducked back behind the rock.

His friends hurried over. But when Laurel saw what lay on the other side of the rock, she froze. A cave! A huge cave, stretching into endless darkness.

"I'm sure the sound came from here," Foxglove said. "The walls of the cave are what made it echo."

Then the voice spoke again. "I hear you out there!" he exclaimed. "Go away, I tell you."

But now the voice sounded even weaker.

"We have to go in there," said Laurel slowly. She tried not to show her fear.

"I'll go," Foxglove said. "Just let me have one of your candles."

Laurel gave the pixie a thankful look. Quickly she took a candle out of her bag and lit it.

Candle in hand, Foxglove stepped into the cave. In a matter of seconds, he was out of sight.

Suddenly a roar came from the cave. "GET OUT OF HERE!"

Laurel gasped and started forward. "Oh, I shouldn't have let Foxglove go in there alone."

"Don't worry," said Mistletoe. "I'll check on him." The mouse ran into the cave.

"And I'll stay here," said Chitters nervously. "Keep Laurel safe. Watch over her!" He darted to Laurel's feet and hid there.

Now Laurel could hear a low mumble from the cave. At least the angry voice had stopped roaring.

Finally Mistletoe came back.

"Where's Foxglove?" asked Laurel.

"He stayed behind," reported Mistletoe. "With the dwarf."

"Dwarf!" exclaimed Laurel. She'd heard of dwarves from Foxglove. But she'd never met one before.

"Yes. And the dwarf is hurt and can't walk. Foxglove asked if you'd come and help."

Laurel started to tremble. The thought of entering that dark cave terrified her.

But if someone needed help, she had no choice.

Laurel straightened her shoulders. Her hands were surprisingly steady as she lit another candle.

The light comforted Laurel a bit. With Mistletoe and Chitters by her side, she bravely made her way into the cave. She tried not to think about the tons and tons of rock that surrounded her. Or about the dark and cold.

Mistletoe glanced up at Laurel. "This way," she said. "Don't worry, Laurel. It's not far."

It seemed far to Laurel. The floor of the cave was rough and rocky. The damp walls closed in on her. Huge rocks hung overhead, looking as though they could fall at any time.

At last she caught sight of Foxglove. The pixie was bent down beside another figure. It was the dwarf.

Laurel almost forgot her fear as she stared in wonder at the little man. He was short—shorter than either Laurel or Foxglove. A simple tunic and pants covered his sturdy frame. And was that fur on his head?

As Laurel got closer, she saw it was actually the dwarf's wild white hair. A long, tangled beard covered his chin and flowed to his waist.

Now the dwarf groaned again and held his knee. But his eyes blazed up at Foxglove. The old fellow looked fearless.

"Oh! You *are* hurt!" cried Laurel. She dropped to her knees beside the dwarf. Then she searched in her bag and took out a scarf. After folding it in half, she reached out.

"DON'T TOUCH—" roared the dwarf. But he stopped when Laurel began wrapping the scarf around his knee.

"This will protect it until we get you out of here," she said softly.

Once the bandage was in place, Laurel and Foxglove helped the dwarf up. Then they led him toward the cave entrance. The dwarf hopped along on his good leg.

"What happened to you?" asked Laurel.

"What happened?" snapped the dwarf. "What happened, indeed! This is your fault, woodfairy! Yours and that pixie's. I climbed onto a rock so I'd be out of sight if you came into the cave. Is it any wonder I slipped?"

Laurel let the old fellow talk. She could feel him tremble and knew he was more shaken than he let on.

"We're sorry," she said. "We didn't mean to bother you."

"Hmmmph!" grunted the old dwarf.

They reached the entrance to the cave. As they stepped out into the welcome light, Laurel breathed a happy sigh. It seemed as if she'd been inside the cave for hours rather than minutes.

Together Laurel and Foxglove eased the dwarf onto the bench. Then Laurel glanced at the iron kettle that hung over the cold ashes. "Foxglove, would you please heat up some water?" she asked. "I'll see what I can do for his knee."

"I think you've done enough already!" fussed the dwarf.

Laurel paid no attention. She untied the scarf bandage and rolled up the leg of the dwarf's heavy woolen pants. The knee was definitely swollen. And there was an old scar running across it.

"You've been hurt before," she said, looking up at the dwarf's face.

"Yes," he said with pride. "An old battle wound. Fighting off the trolls."

"Ah," said Laurel. "I've met the trolls. You must be very brave if you've done battle with them."

The dwarf's frown faded just a bit. "It was nothing any dwarf wouldn't have done."

Laurel called Mistletoe over to her. The mouse listened closely. "I think I know where to find some," she told Laurel.

After the kettle had heated, Laurel dipped a soft cloth in the warm water. Then she wrapped the dwarf's knee with the cloth. By the time she finished, Mistletoe was back. The mouse held a leafy plant in her mouth.

"Thanks, Mistletoe," said Laurel. She turned to the dwarf. "Now I'm going to make you some tea. It will help with the pain."

An hour later, the dwarf sat with his bandaged leg up on a tree stump. An empty teacup sat on the bench next to him. In his lap was a half-eaten bowl of berries.

The others were eating too. And they were enjoying the peace and quiet.

At least he's stopped shouting at us, thought Laurel. She glanced at the dwarf. He didn't look cheerful. But the lines of pain had disappeared from his face.

"We've told you our names," she said. "But we still don't know yours."

The old dwarf was silent for a time. Then he cleared his throat and announced, "My name is Boden."

Laurel nodded. "We're pleased to meet you, Boden." She poked Foxglove, who quickly agreed.

The dwarf's eyes darted first to Laurel's face, then Foxglove's. "So my name isn't known to you?"

Laurel glanced at Foxglove. He just shrugged. Laurel turned back to the dwarf. "I don't recognize it," she said. "But I've never known any dwarves before."

"Just as well," muttered Boden. Then his voice turned cold. "Now you know my name. And that's all you need to know. It's time you were on your way."

Foxglove looked up. "But—" he began.

Laurel quickly broke in. In a soft voice, she said, "Boden, it's getting late. Surely you wouldn't have us climb that cliff in the dark?"

The dwarf fixed his eyes on the sky. At last he said, "And no moon out tonight. Well, it's not the dwarf way to put another in danger. So I suppose you may stay."

"Thank you," said Laurel.

"But only tonight," Boden added. "In the morning, I expect you to be on your way!"

"We understand," replied Laurel. However, Foxglove noticed that she hadn't exactly promised to do as the dwarf asked.

Evening fell over the glade. The mountains and trees cast long shadows across the valley. Laurel leaned closer to the fire as the last daylight slipped away. "What a lovely night," she said. "Everything seems so still and peaceful here in your glade. As if the world were far, far away."

"The world *is* far away," Boden said. He stared at the fire for a few moments. "And it *is* peaceful here," he continued at last. "Or at least it was until you came."

Laurel and her friends were silent after that. Finally Boden stirred. He began to speak—almost as if he were talking to himself. "It reminds me of a night long ago," he said. Then he paused.

Laurel sensed a story coming. She didn't want Boden to stop now. "A night long ago?" she asked.

"Yes. A night that became part of dwarf history…"

As he told his tale, Boden seemed to forget where he was. He spoke of the first time that he'd visited Tarmok. It was the dream of every dwarf to climb that mighty mountain. But none had ever made it to the top.

Even so, Boden and his friends decided to try. They reached the mountain at sunset and made camp at its base. All that night, they sang and told stories of Tarmok. And as the sun rose,

40

they headed up the mountain.

They spent two days climbing, finally reaching the top. But with all the glories of the climb, Boden's favorite night was still the first one. The night he and his friends camped at the mountain's base and celebrated Tarmok.

Laurel was fascinated. This is what history should be like, she thought. Stories that told about how people felt!

When the dwarf finished, Laurel clapped. "That was just wonderful!" she cried. "Can you tell us another?"

Boden blinked. "Another? I think not," he said. He lowered his head onto his chest and stared at the fire. "I don't know what came over me…"

"Instead of telling more stories, perhaps you'd answer some questions," suggested Foxglove.

"Perhaps," said Boden.

"Is this place known as the Deeps?" Foxglove asked.

The dwarf stared at the pixie. Slowly he nodded.

"We've heard a story about the Deeps," said Foxglove. "There's talk of a treasure hidden here. Do you know anything about it?"

At the word "treasure," the dwarf forgot his knee and jumped to his feet. His mouth tightened with pain. "Who told you about a treasure?" he exploded.

"The forest animals," Foxglove announced.

"Animals? Talking?" snorted the dwarf.

"Yes, just like Chitters and Mistletoe," replied Foxglove.

The dwarf swung around to stare at the chipmunk and mouse. "I don't believe it!" he shouted.

"It's true," Laurel told him. "All animals talk."

The dwarf turned to her. "I don't believe it, I said! What silliness! Animals talking. Treasure in the Deeps. Well, there's no treasure here for you."

Foxglove opened his mouth to ask another question. But Laurel placed a hand on the pixie's arm and shook her head. Foxglove shrugged and Boden settled back in his seat.

This time no one broke the silence. And before long, the tired old dwarf fell asleep. Laurel and Foxglove covered him with a blanket.

"Did you see how mad he got when I asked about the treasure?" whispered Foxglove. "He's looking for it too!"

"I don't know about that," said Laurel. "But there's some mystery about him. For one thing, what's he doing out here all by himself?"

"I've been wondering about that," admitted Foxglove. "Dwarves are close to their families. They never live alone."

"Maybe we can find some answers in the morning," said Laurel. "For now, we'd better get some rest."

They lay down by the fire. Mistletoe and Chitters curled up near Laurel. Soon the four explorers had joined the old dwarf in sleep.

～

"Still here, are you?"

The crabby voice woke Laurel. She sat up. Foxglove was stirring too. Mistletoe and Chitters were already awake and keeping a watchful eye on Boden.

The old dwarf was standing by the dead fire. He leaned on a stick and frowned down at Laurel and her friends.

"The sun's long up," he said. "Time you were moving!"

Laurel got to her feet. "You look better today," she said.

The dwarf curled his lip. "A little fall never killed a dwarf." Then he added, "And now I'm off. Some of us have

42

work to do."

With that, he limped toward the cave. Halfway there Boden turned. "I expect you all to be gone when I return," he warned.

"Be careful!" was Laurel's only reply.

Foxglove sat up. "Well, I refuse to be chased off," he said. "Not when I'm this close to the treasure."

"You can't be sure of that," replied Laurel.

"I can feel it!" said Foxglove. "The treasure's nearby. And that old dwarf wants to beat me to it. I've got to find it before he does. So I'm not leaving now!"

"Foxglove, please calm down!" Laurel cried.

The pixie looked a little ashamed of himself. "All right. Sorry," he mumbled.

"In any case, I don't think we should leave," added Laurel.

"What?" asked Mistletoe and Chitters, their ears twitching.

Foxglove stared at Laurel. "You don't? But I thought you didn't want me to go into any caves."

"That's right," said Laurel calmly. "I'm not saying we should stay because of the treasure. I'm worried about Boden. I think he needs our help."

Foxglove shook his head. "He may *need* our help. But he certainly doesn't *want* it."

Even as he spoke, Foxglove knew that Laurel was planning something. And he knew that her plans had nothing to do with finding treasure.

"Okay," he sighed. "Tell me what you've got in mind."

Laurel broke into a big smile. "Just listen to this idea!" she said.

CHAPTER SEVEN

The Downfall of a King

'm listening," said Foxglove. "But don't try to talk me out of hunting for the treasure."

"Let's hear your plan, Laurel," said Mistletoe.

"I think we should fix up this place," suggested Laurel proudly.

"What?" said her three friends in one voice.

Foxglove jumped up. "Boden doesn't even want us here!"

"That's what he says. But I'm sure that's not how he really feels," said Laurel.

Chitters started to grumble. "He's mean. Really mean! Why help him?"

"He's not mean," argued Laurel. "Just a little crabby."

Foxglove laughed. "A *little* crabby?"

Laurel continued. "I think it's because he's sad and lonely. I want to help him. Make him feel more comfortable. And I want to show him that we care."

Her three friends were quiet. At last Foxglove sighed. "Fine. Tell us what you want us to do. The sooner we finish, the sooner I can go treasure hunting!"

So Laurel explained. Foxglove complained a bit. But in the end, he agreed.

The four friends set to work. All morning they came and went from forest to glade and glade to forest. A few times,

Foxglove wandered off to stare longingly at the cave. But each time, Laurel found him and gave him another chore.

By late afternoon, they had finished. The four stepped back to study their work. Even Foxglove was proud of what they had done.

The clearing looked totally different. The rocky soil around the campfire had been swept clean. A hammock made from soft vines hung between two trees. And within sight of the fire stood a lovely trellis made from branches.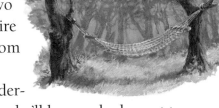

"Let's put Boden's chair underneath the trellis," Laurel said. "Then he'll have a shady spot to sit."

So they did. Laurel nodded. "It's perfect," she sighed.

"I certainly hope he likes this," said Foxglove.

"He will," Laurel said. "Though he may not tell us."

Then she started looking through Boden's food supply. "Let's see what we can cook up for dinner. I think Boden could use a good meal."

"I'll do that," said Foxglove. "All this work has made me hungry."

He sent Laurel and the two animals to collect nuts and wild mushrooms. Foxglove added these to dried beans from Boden's pack. In no time, a kettle of delicious stew bubbled over the fire.

Finally the pixie threw himself down on the soft grass. "That's it!" he said. "I'm not doing one more thing."

"Are you sure?" asked Laurel with a smile. "Not even a little exploring?"

"What do you mean?" asked Foxglove.

"I thought we'd take a look around the cave," she replied. She added quickly, "Not inside. Just near the entrance."

"Fine," said Foxglove, grabbing his scavenging bag. "I'm too tired to do much more than that anyway!"

Laurel turned to the two animals. "Are you coming along?"

"I wouldn't want to miss out on the fun," said Mistletoe.

"Me too! Absolutely! Without a doubt!" said Chitters.

Foxglove led the way. Soon all four were carefully studying the rocks in front of the cave. Foxglove even went inside—back to the spot where he'd found Boden.

"No signs of treasure," the pixie said when he came out into the open again. "And that's enough exploring for me today." He lay down on top of a flat rock.

Laurel, Chitters, and Mistletoe joined him. They all needed a rest after their hard day's work. For a while, they sat and enjoyed the warmth of the late afternoon's pale sunshine.

"Tomorrow I'm going deeper into the cave," Foxglove said. "So don't try to stop me. I know Boden's looking for the treasure. And he already has a head start!"

Laurel sighed. "I know, I know. But I can't help worrying what might happen if you go too far into that cave. And I don't understand how Boden can go in there all by himself."

"Dwarves are miners," said Foxglove. "For them, rocks and caves are like trees and forests are to you."

At that moment, they heard a noise. "I think he's coming," said Laurel.

"And he's not going to be happy to see us, I'm afraid," groaned Foxglove.

The pixie was right. The old dwarf appeared, leaning heavily on his stick. He paused to wipe the gray dust from his beard and clothing. As he straightened up, he saw Laurel and her friends.

"YOU!" he shouted. He started to wave his stick. But he was too tired. As soon as he lifted the stick, his old legs gave out.

"Oh, Boden!" cried Laurel as she hurried to his side. "I knew you shouldn't be in there working all by yourself!"

"What are you still doing here?" snapped Boden. "You were all supposed to be gone by now!"

In spite of his words, Boden took Laurel's arm and held on tightly. "Well, as long as you're here, the two of you can help me over these rocks," he said.

So with Laurel and Foxglove at his side, Boden limped back to camp. It was clear that the old fellow was worn out.

When they reached the glade, Boden stopped cold. His eyes took in the bubbling kettle. Then he saw the trellis and the vine hammock.

"What...why...how?" he stammered. He finally found his tongue. "In the name of the seven mountains, what happened here?"

"Do you like it?" asked Laurel softly.

"Like it? Do I like it?" Boden shook his head slowly. Then he growled, "I didn't ask for help, you know!"

"No," said Laurel. "You didn't ask."

Boden shook his head again. "I don't need your help. I don't even want you here." But the tone of his voice didn't match his angry words. With wonder in his eyes, he touched the trellis.

Foxglove helped the old fellow ease into his chair. "There you are," said Laurel. "You can see the fire from here."

"So I can," said Boden softly. "So I can."

He looked around the glade once more. Then he said, "I

didn't ask for help. But it's fine work you do—for a pixie and a woodfairy. And a mouse and chipmunk," he added with a nod to the two animals. "As fine as a dwarf can do, it is."

Laurel knew that this was high praise indeed. But she didn't say anything. She just went ahead and took care of Boden's knee. Meanwhile, Foxglove filled bowls with food.

After his third helping of stew, Boden finally set his bowl down. Knitting his brows together, he fixed his eyes on Laurel and Foxglove. "I suppose it's too late for you to leave—again," he said.

"What do you think we should do?" Laurel asked.

"I guess you'd better stay another night," the old dwarf said. "It wouldn't be right to send you off now."

"Thank you," said Laurel. "We'd love to stay." She winked at Foxglove. The pixie had to turn away before Boden saw his smile.

It slowly grew dark. At first everyone sat quietly, staring into the fire. Then Laurel said, "Boden, would you tell us another story?"

The dwarf had almost fallen asleep. Now his head jerked upright. "Another story?" he said. "More of my wandering words, you mean?"

"Oh, Boden," Laurel objected. "Your story last night was wonderful. And you told it exactly right! The way I wish woodfairy history was told!"

Boden couldn't hide his satisfaction. "Hmmm. Well, I guess I know another tale or two." He sat back and thought for a moment. A look of sadness came over his face, and he nodded. "Yes. I know just the story to tell."

Laurel reached for her traveling bag. "Is it all right if I write it down while you talk?"

Boden looked surprised. "Write it down? You mean you're going to write my words?"

"Yes," said Laurel. She took her journal out of her bag and showed it to the dwarf. "This is my journal. Every woodfairy has one. We record what happens to us each day."

Boden studied the book. "We dwarves keep our records here," he said, pointing to his head. "But suit yourself. Write if you want to."

The old dwarf settled himself comfortably in his chair. Then, in his deep, booming voice, he unfolded his story.

This is the tale of the downfall of a great dwarf king. Or at least of a king who once thought he was great.

You may know that dwarves are craftspeople. We make lovely things from gold and silver, jewels and crystal. We take the treasures of the earth and free their beauty.

But there came a time when our treasures began to vanish! A jeweled cup here. A necklace there. And never any sign of the thieves.

Yet for all that, it was easy to guess who was to blame. It had to be trolls! The evil trolls are always after dwarf treasure.

We had to find out how the thieves were sneaking into Dwarf Hall. Until then nothing would be safe. Not even our most important treasure—the Jewels of Shona.

Queen Shona ruled the dwarves long ago. Before her time, we grubbed and grasped for gold. She helped us see that things shouldn't be valued for the price they brought. Instead, they should be valued for their beauty, meaning, and history. We began to take joy in sharing and passing down our treasures.

The Jewels of Shona were the queen's gifts to us. Every piece was special in its own way. And each told a part of dwarf history. You can understand why that treasure was so important. And why we didn't want the trolls to ever get their hands on it.

As the thefts continued, we became more worried. The king met with his closest advisors. They talked about how to protect the Jewels of Shona. But they couldn't agree.

The king was a stubborn old man. He thought his was the only way. He wanted to take the jewels and hide them deep in a cavern. A cavern that had been mined years ago, then deserted. The treasure would be safe there!

The advisors argued with the king. The cavern was too far away, they said. And it wasn't safe. It would be better to keep the treasure in Dwarf Hall. There it could be protected night and day. At the same time, guards would watch for the trolls.

But the king wouldn't listen. One dark night, he gathered up the Jewels of Shona. Then he sent for his trusted servants. They moved the treasure to the cavern.

Several nights later, two trolls were spotted. They were followed to a hidden tunnel at the edge of the mountain. And the tunnel led into Dwarf Hall.

The guards quickly set to work and blocked the tunnel. When they were finished, even the strongest troll couldn't have gotten through.

And now the king realized that he hadn't needed to hide the treasure after all. He told his advisors what he had done and promised to bring the jewels back to Dwarf Hall.

The king and his soldiers returned to the caverns to get the treasure. There they made an awful discovery. It had been raining for days, and the caverns were flooded!

They waited for the water to go down. But when they finally got inside, they found that the flood had caused a cave-in. A wall of rock blocked them from the cavern where the treasure was hidden.

The king and his soldiers started to dig. But it was impossible. Every time a rock was removed, the chance of another cave-in became greater.

The king knew he couldn't put his soldiers in danger. So he stopped the digging. He and his soldiers returned home empty-handed. And the king had to admit that he had lost the Jewels of Shona.

The king could no longer face his people. In the end, he turned the throne over to his daughter. And from then on, he lived in shame.

Boden's voice trailed off. He sat and stared into the dying fire.

"Is that the end of the story?" asked Foxglove.

"Yes," said Boden in a whisper.

"But it's so sad!" exclaimed Laurel.

"Very sad," agreed Boden.

"And unfair too!" said Foxglove. "The king just made a simple mistake. Everybody makes mistakes! Why did he have to spend the rest of his life in shame?"

"But it wasn't just a simple mistake," explained Boden. "He was too stubborn and too proud to listen to others. And his pride led to a terrible loss. One felt by every dwarf in the kingdom."

A moment of silence fell over the group.

"And now," said Boden, "I'm very tired. It's time I went to bed."

Laurel and Foxglove helped the old dwarf to his vine hammock. He was soon sound asleep. Even in sleep, his face wore a look of sadness.

Mistletoe and Chitters settled down too. But Laurel and

Foxglove sat up talking for a little longer.

"At least now we know more about the treasure," said Foxglove. "It has to be the one the dwarf king lost."

"Yes," said Laurel. "And now we also know why Boden is so lonely and unhappy."

"You mean because he's trying to get the treasure back? And he hasn't been able to?" said Foxglove.

"I mean because he feels he failed his people."

Foxglove stared at her. "Laurel, are you saying...?"

"I'm saying that Boden is the old dwarf king," replied Laurel.

CHAPTER EIGHT

Danger in the Deeps

aurel opened her eyes. It was daylight, but the sky was gray and overcast. A fine rain was just beginning to fall.

She sat up and looked around the camp. Foxglove was still sleeping, and so were Mistletoe and Chitters. Laurel glanced over at the hammock to check on Boden.

The dwarf's blanket was neatly folded and tucked under the table to keep it dry. Boden himself was nowhere in sight.

"Oh no," sighed Laurel. "He's gone into the cave again!"

Foxglove opened his eyes. "He's gone?" he said. Then he looked up at the cloudy sky. "I wouldn't worry, Laurel. Boden is probably drier in that cave than we are out here."

He sat up when he remembered what Laurel had said just before falling asleep. "Laurel, do you still believe what you said last night? Do you really think that Boden is the old king of the dwarves?"

"He has to be," said Laurel. "Don't you see? That's why he's living here all by himself. And working so hard in the cave. He's trying to get the treasure back for his people."

Foxglove thought for a bit. Then he shook his head. "I don't know, Laurel. He doesn't seem much like a king to me."

Laurel put her hands on her hips. For a long time, she just stared at the pixie. Finally Foxglove dropped his eyes. "Okay,

okay! You're probably right," he said.

"And…" said Laurel.

Foxglove sighed a long, deep sigh. "And that means I can't scavenge this treasure. Not if it belongs to Boden and the dwarves."

Laurel smiled. Now Foxglove was beginning to sound like his old self.

The pixie slowly got to his feet. Just as slowly, he reached for his scavenging bag. "We might as well go," he announced. "There's no point in staying here now. I can't scavenge the treasure. We've already fixed up the campsite. And Boden doesn't want us around."

"I don't know," said Laurel. "I still don't like the idea of leaving him here alone." She started piling things under the trees, out of the rain. "I want to stay at least one more day. When Boden comes out tonight, I'll talk to him. Maybe I can get him to go home."

Foxglove looked off into the distance. Even the tallest, rockiest mountain seemed friendlier to him than Boden. But Foxglove owed this to Laurel. She'd stuck by him earlier.

"All right," he said. "We'll stay. But only one more day."

The little group ate a late breakfast. Then they got busy. Mistletoe and Chitters looked for food. Laurel and Foxglove gathered firewood.

They had just sat down to rest when a rushing sound filled the air. "What's that?" asked Laurel.

She soon had an answer to her question. The sky darkened as hundreds and hundreds of bats darted overhead. They were coming from the direction of the cave.

"Bats!" cried Foxglove. "What are they doing out now?"

"Shhh!" said Laurel. "They're talking. I'm trying to hear what they're saying."

She struggled to understand the high-pitched sounds. At last she made out a few words.

"Foxglove! Something is wrong!"

"I know," replied the pixie. "Bats never fly during the day."

"I think they were saying something about a flood!" Laurel exclaimed.

"A flood?" repeated Foxglove. He gave a worried look at the sky. "It's all this rain."

"Exactly," agreed Laurel. "I think the cave is going to flood. Just like it did the time the treasure got buried!"

"And Boden is in there!" exclaimed Foxglove.

"We have to warn him," said Laurel.

"That means going into the cave," Foxglove pointed out.

"I know," replied Laurel. She sounded calm. But Foxglove could see that she was frightened.

"We'll come too," said Mistletoe.

Laurel smiled slightly. "Good. You can use your noses to help us find Boden."

The four headed straight to the cave. Just inside, they found two torches that the old dwarf had left by the entrance. "Thank goodness," sighed Laurel when she saw them. Foxglove held the torches while Laurel lit them. Then Laurel took one.

The faint light of the torches did little to erase Laurel's fears. Her hand shook. And so did her voice.

Foxglove glanced at her. "Are you sure you want to do

this?" he asked. "You could wait here."

"And worry about all of you?" objected Laurel. "No, it's better if I come along." She fluttered her wings nervously. "Now let's go. Before I change my mind."

Mistletoe and Chitters led the way, sniffing for the dwarf's scent. Laurel and Foxglove followed, their torches held high. The dancing flames cast strange shadows on the rough walls of the cave. But at least they gave off more light than candles would.

It wasn't far to the small chamber where Foxglove had first found Boden. Just beyond, there was a fork in the cave. Old mine tunnels ran off to the left and right. The torchlight barely touched the blackness of these tunnels. And there was nothing to show which way Boden had gone.

"No clues here," said Laurel.

"Let's see if I can help," said Mistletoe. She put her sharp little nose to the floor. "It's hard to tell for sure," the mouse said. "The rocks don't hold scents very well. But I think he might have gone this way." She headed to the left.

"Yes! Yes! Let's go!" cried Chitters. He raced off behind Mistletoe. Laurel and Foxglove followed.

They walked on in silence. Laurel's knees felt weak and her heart beat fast, but she kept going.

After a while, the tunnel began to slope downward. In places water dripped down the cave walls. It pooled underfoot and made the floor slippery.

Puddles weren't the only problem. Mistletoe and Chitters stopped and quickly compared notes. "We can't smell Boden anymore," squeaked Mistletoe. "Either the water washed his scent away, or he hasn't been here lately."

"Do you think we should turn back?" asked Foxglove.

"We could try the other tunnel."

"Let's go a bit farther," said Laurel. "Maybe they'll catch his scent again."

Then she noticed a line on the wall just over her head. The rock was darker below the line than it was above.

Laurel pointed it out to Foxglove. "What do you think that line means?" she asked.

Foxglove stopped and studied the wall. "Nothing good," he said at last. "I think it shows how high the water rose last time the cave flooded."

"That high?" questioned Laurel. She felt a chill run up her spine. "We've got to find Boden! As soon as we can!"

"I just hope we're headed in the right direction," sighed Foxglove.

They continued on their way, but it was hard to make much speed. The tunnel narrowed and its roof became lower. In some spots, Laurel and Foxglove had to duck to keep from hitting their heads.

Then the tunnel curved sharply to the right. Mistletoe rounded the corner and let out a squeak of surprise.

Laurel, Foxglove, and Chitters hurried to catch up. When they reached Mistletoe, they too gasped in wonder.

In front of them, the tunnel opened up into a huge underground room. Ribbons of water ran down the walls and flowed into a deep lake. And rocks every color of the rainbow gleamed from the walls.

Laurel stepped farther in and stared up at the ceiling high above. Like the walls, it was dotted with colorful rocks.

Laurel spun around. As she did, the flames of her torch reflected off the walls and ceiling. Sparks of yellow, white, and blue flashed through the air. For a moment, the beauty of it all

made her forget her fear.

"It's like floating in a pool of light!" exclaimed Laurel. "It's glorious."

"Glorious!" echoed Chitters.

Meanwhile, Mistletoe was exploring, nose to the floor. "I can't pick up Boden's scent," she called.

Chitters tore his eyes away from the dancing light and sniffed too. "Nothing! Not a thing!" he announced.

"Well, you two keep checking," said Foxglove. "We'll look over here." He hurried off toward the other side of the great underground room.

"Wait for me," called Laurel. But the pixie was far ahead of her. As Laurel watched, he disappeared into a narrow opening in the far wall.

"Foxglove," she cried. "What do you think you're doing?" She ran toward the opening and slipped through.

Just ahead Laurel could see Foxglove's torch bobbing up and down. The pixie was making his way across a wide bridge of rock. Below the bridge was a dark, bottomless pit.

Laurel couldn't believe her eyes. Foxglove hated high places. Yet here he was, walking along as if he were on a path through the forest.

"Foxglove!" she called in a low voice. "Stop right there!"

The pixie paused and looked back. "Come on, Laurel," he called. "It's perfectly safe." He pointed to an opening at the other end of the rock bridge. "I'll bet you anything that this is the way to Boden and his treasure."

Laurel stepped out onto the bridge. It certainly didn't look safe to her. She had to get to her friend and make him come back!

Suddenly she heard a loud, cracking noise. A sharp gasp

followed. Foxglove's torch tumbled into the darkness.

"What happened?" Laurel cried.

"Don't come any closer!" shouted Foxglove. But his warning came too late. Laurel felt the rock beneath her feet shift. The bridge was falling!

Her torch fell at her feet. Laurel looked about wildly. Along the wall, she saw several narrow ledges sticking out.

"Jump!" She screamed. "To the ledge!"

Foxglove didn't stop to ask questions. He leapt off the bridge onto a long shelf of rock. Laurel followed.

They barely made it. Most of the bridge crumbled and dropped noisily from sight. Laurel's torch fell along with it, leaving them in complete darkness.

For a long time, neither one of them spoke or moved. Then Laurel carefully stretched out one foot.

The edge of the rock shelf was only inches away. In a panic, Laurel pressed herself against the wall.

"Can you can fly back to the opening?" asked Foxglove.

"I don't know," said Laurel doubtfully. "It's too dark to see anything. And my wings are all wet and muddy."

Laurel took a deep breath. Then she fluttered her wings as hard as she could. Slowly she rose into the air. But the weight of her wet wings quickly dragged her down.

"It's no use," she sobbed. "I can't! And even if I could, I wouldn't be able to get you out."

"Don't worry about that," moaned Foxglove. "It's my fault we're in this mess."

"Shhh!" whispered Laurel. "Listen!"

They heard faint squeaks and trills calling their names.

"Mistletoe! Chitters!" Laurel shouted. "We're over here!"

"We're stuck!" Foxglove added. "Go and get some help!"

"All right," came the faint voices. "We'll be back!"

Laurel and Foxglove sank down on the ledge. For a moment, neither said a word. Then Laurel spoke softly. "We can count on Chitters and Mistletoe," she said. "They'll do something."

"What can they do?" asked Foxglove sadly. "Even if they find Boden, they can't talk to him."

Laurel had no answer to that. The two friends leaned close to one another. With thundering hearts, they waited in the darkness.

CHAPTER NINE

To the Rescue!

Chitters raced back along the tunnel. "Help! Help! Please help!"

Mistletoe charged after him. "Chitters!" she called. "Wait for me!"

The chipmunk slowed down. "Save them! Must save them!" he panted.

"Of course," Mistletoe agreed. "But first we have to find Boden. And then we have to make him understand us."

"Where? How?" cried Chitters.

"This way," said Mistletoe. She moved into the lead, hurrying back to the fork in the tunnel. From there she dashed down the tunnel to the right.

A few feet inside, Mistletoe suddenly stopped. She sniffed the air. "This is the way," she announced. "If only we'd gone down this tunnel first!"

"Hurry! Hurry! Hurry!" shouted Chitters. The chipmunk waved his tail and took off.

Mistletoe and Chitters made good time. They were small enough to run along a dry, smooth ledge at the side of the tunnel.

At last they heard banging and crashing noises. Those sounds were followed by grunts. Boden had to be just ahead.

"Come on!" called Mistletoe. She zipped around the next

corner. The tunnel widened and suddenly came to an end. A huge pile of rocks blocked the way.

And there was Boden. He was working by the light of a single lantern. Every crash of his pick shook the lantern—and the tunnel itself.

Mistletoe sat up. "Boden!" she squeaked.

But the old dwarf was making such a racket that he didn't hear.

Chitters ran to the top of a rock pile. Chattering wildly, he threw himself at the dwarf.

"By the seven mountains!" cried Boden as he felt something land on his head. "It's a cave-in!" But when he reached up, he discovered only an excited ball of fur.

The old dwarf lowered the chipmunk to eye level. "You!" he cried. "What are you doing here? Be off with you!"

Boden jumped as he felt something attack his ankle. "It's the other one!" he grumbled when he saw Mistletoe. He turned to look for Laurel and Foxglove.

Chitters took that opportunity to climb onto one of Boden's shoulders. And Mistletoe climbed onto the other. The animals began jabbering away.

"Enough!" cried Boden.

Mistletoe and Chitters stopped. The dwarf removed the animals and placed them on a rock. "Now then, what's going on?" he asked.

The two animals began to squeak and chatter. But Boden hushed them. "That's no good," he growled. "I can't understand you! I've never mastered such woodfairy foolishness!"

Chitters and Mistletoe talked to each other for a moment. Then they jumped to the ground. Mistletoe took one of Boden's pant legs between her teeth and tugged.

"Do you want me to follow you?" asked Boden. Chitters ran down the tunnel a bit. Then he sat and waited.

"Yes, you do!" said Boden. An awful thought hit him. "There's something wrong with Laurel, isn't there? And that little pixie."

Boden muttered to himself. "I knew they'd be a bother. Keeping me from my work. I told them to leave. But they had to stay!"

Yet Boden looked more worried than angry. He grabbed a torch and his walking stick. With these in hand, he turned to the animals. "Show me where they are!"

Mistletoe and Chitters took off. Boden followed, moving as fast as his sore knee would let him.

They made their way back through the tunnel. Finally they arrived at the fork, where the tunnel split into two branches. When Boden saw Mistletoe and Chitters head to the left, he groaned. "Oh no! They're here in the cave!"

The old dwarf moved faster now. His breath came in gasps, and he stumbled from time to time.

At last they reached the huge underground room. As Boden hurried toward the narrow opening, he whispered, "Worse and worse. Just don't let me be too late."

Mistletoe and Chitters reached the opening first. The old dwarf struggled through behind them. Mistletoe cried, "Laurel! Foxglove! We're back! And Boden's with us!"

Boden's torch lit up a terrible sight. Across from him, Laurel and Foxglove were standing on a shelf of rock. Between them and safety lay a huge stretch of empty space.

"Just stay put!" Boden called. "I'll get you out of there."

The old dwarf leaned his torch against a rock. For several moments, he studied the cave wall above the shelf of rock. Finally he untied a thick rope that hung from his belt.

Laurel and Foxglove watched as Boden made a loop at one end of the rope. Then he swung it around his head in ever-widening circles. It sailed out into the air—and right past them.

Boden pulled the rope back. Once again he swung it in circles. This time the loop settled over a rock high above Laurel and Foxglove.

The dwarf swung the other end of the rope over to them. "Pull on it!" he ordered. "Make sure it's good and tight."

Laurel reached out and grabbed the rope. She pulled as hard as she could.

"It's tight!" she called.

Boden shouted directions to her. "Back up as far as you can," he said. "Then run forward and swing over to me. Come on!"

Laurel took a long, deep breath before following Boden's instructions. She sailed out into space, flapping her wings for balance. In a matter of seconds, she had reached the end of the bridge. Mistletoe and Chitters cheered loudly.

Boden swung the rope back to the waiting pixie. "Now you, Foxglove," he shouted.

Foxglove took the rope in both hands. He backed up and ran forward, just as Laurel had done. But at the very edge of the rock, he stopped and peered fearfully down.

"Don't think about it!" cried Laurel.

Foxglove backed up and tried again. This time he closed his eyes when he reached the edge. With a frightened cry, he flew across the space.

"Ooof!" Foxglove landed on the rocks with a loud thud. For a second, he lay there. Then Boden helped him to his feet.

"Let's get out of here before the rest of this bridge falls," the dwarf muttered.

When they were safely in the cavern, Laurel turned to the old dwarf. "Oh, Boden, thank you. If it weren't for you—"

Boden banged his walking stick on the rock floor. "Indeed! And just what are you doing in here? I told you to stay out! I told you to leave! Don't you know how dangerous this cave is?"

Foxglove hung his head. He quietly said, "It was all my fault, Boden. And you're right. I was foolish."

"But we were looking for you," added Laurel. "We had to warn you."

"Warn me!" snorted the dwarf. "Seems to me that you're the ones who need warning."

"You don't understand!" said Laurel. "The cave is starting to flood! You can't work in here anymore!"

A stubborn look came over the dwarf's face. "I have to!" he objected. "I know the caves are flooding. And that's why I have to hurry. I must finish before the Deeps are completely flooded!"

Boden grabbed his torch. Turning to Foxglove and Laurel, he snapped. "Enough talking! It's high time I returned to my work."

But the hurried trip through the tunnels had worn him out. As the old dwarf started back, he stumbled. His tired legs folded beneath him.

Laurel and Foxglove both moved at the same time. They caught Boden by the elbows.

"Come on," said Foxglove. "Let's get you out of here."

"But my work…" Boden said weakly.

"Must wait until you've rested," Laurel finished for him.

Boden frowned. At last he gave in. "Very well."

With Mistletoe and Chitters dashing ahead of them, they headed down the tunnel. When they at last made it out of the cave, Laurel paused. She lifted her face to the cold rain. "I don't think I've ever been so glad to see clouds," she said.

"I know what you mean," replied Foxglove.

"Well, I would prefer a warm fire," Boden declared.

Laurel and Foxglove took the hint. They helped the dwarf to his chair. Then, beneath the trees, they lit a campfire. All five sat motionless, watching the smoke circle and drift in its own tiny clouds.

Finally Laurel took a deep breath. "Boden, please listen to me. It's really too dangerous to be in that cave." She told the dwarf about the whispers she had heard from the bats.

"I'm not listening to bats," grumbled Boden. "Or wood-fairies and pixies either." In a low voice, he added, "I know what I have to do. And I'll do it. Even if it costs me my life."

Laurel sighed. But she knew Boden was too tired to go back into the cave right away. So she'd worry about stopping him in the morning.

"Let's have something to eat," she suggested.

"Sounds wonderful," Foxglove agreed.

Between fixing supper and eating it, they were able to avoid talking about the cave. And not long after their meal, they all went to bed.

Laurel was surprised when Boden said in a kind voice, "Good night."

Almost without thinking, she replied, "Good night, your majesty."

Boden stared at her for several long seconds. At last he nodded and settled back for the night.

～

When Laurel awoke the next morning, the rain was still falling. A quick glance told her that her three friends were already up and about. But Boden was asleep. "Thank goodness!" she whispered. At least the old dwarf hadn't vanished into the cave again.

Foxglove appeared. "Good morning," he said quietly. He emptied his pockets, dumping some berries into a bowl. "Sorry, but it looks like this is it for breakfast today."

"Where are Mistletoe and Chitters?" Laurel asked.

"Out scouting," reported Foxglove. He motioned toward the dwarf. "At least Boden didn't go anywhere."

"Maybe he did listen to us, after all."

"I wouldn't count on it," said Foxglove. "That old fellow is the most stubborn character I've ever met."

"I may be old and stubborn, but there's nothing wrong with my hearing."

Foxglove jumped a bit at the sound of the dwarf's voice.

Boden slowly got to his feet. He reached into his backpack and pulled out a package. "Here," he said gruffly. "This might round out your breakfast."

He handed each of them a hard biscuit. "This is what we dwarves take down into the mines with us," he said. "Nothing can spoil it." He chuckled. "Not even a cave-in!"

Laurel took a tiny nibble. The biscuit was as hard as rock. But the little piece she broke off tasted delicious.

"Thank you," she said.

"No need to thank me," muttered Boden. "You gave me some food. Now I'm doing the same for you. That's all."

The three sat and chewed quietly. It took a long time to eat the hard biscuits. But they were wonderfully filling.

By the time they finished, the rain had let up a bit. However, the sky was still cloud-filled. It looked like it was going to rain off and on all day.

Laurel kept a worried eye on Boden. Was he going to try to go back into the cave?

The dwarf cleared his throat. "I'd better—"

At that moment, Chitters and Mistletoe came racing into the glade. "There's an army coming!" cried Mistletoe. "Dozens of dwarves!"

"Dozens and dozens and dozens," trilled Chitters.

"What are they jabbering about now?" asked Boden.

"There's an army of dwarves coming!" said Foxglove.

"No!" muttered Boden. "I can't let them stop me!"

But Laurel didn't hear the old dwarf. Her attention was on the animals. "Tell me exactly what you saw," she ordered.

"Swords! Spears! Sharp things!" cried Chitters.

"That's right!" said Mistletoe. "They have swords and spears. And they're headed this way!"

"Maybe Boden knows what's going on," said Laurel. She and Foxglove turned to the old dwarf.

He was gone. There was no sign of him anywhere.

"Boden!" Laurel called out. "Boden, where are—"

Her voice was swallowed up in the clatter of weapons. The army burst through the trees! They were surrounded!

CHAPTER TEN

The Search Party

aurel and Foxglove stood back-to-back with Chitters and Mistletoe at their feet.

Laurel could feel Foxglove shaking. She knew he was as terrified as she was. But then the pixie reached for her hand. At least I'm not alone, thought Laurel.

She stared at the army of dwarves that formed a ring around them. The only sound in the glade was the rattle of spears.

Laurel found the courage to speak. "Who are you?" she asked bravely. "And what do you want with us?"

"We'll ask the questions!" barked a soldier.

Laurel fell silent. Why were they so angry? Then she remembered Boden. He'd run off as soon as the dwarf army appeared. Had the dwarves come to punish him for losing the treasure? She couldn't let anything happen to the old fellow!

But she knew an army wasn't the only danger Boden faced. Not if he had gone back into the cave. It had rained all night. The cave must be even more flooded by now!

Laurel forgot about the spears pointed at her. She stepped forward. "Please listen to me," she begged. "If you're looking for

71

Boden—"

"Boden!" cried the dwarves. The name flew from soldier to soldier.

Suddenly the circle of soldiers parted. Out stepped a young dwarf with long, curly hair. Her rich robe was belted with a golden chain. And she was as well armed as the rest of the dwarves.

"What have you done with Boden?" the newcomer asked in an angry voice.

Laurel shook her head. "We haven't done anything with him."

Foxglove jumped in. "We certainly haven't. But we've done a lot *for* him. Fixed up this glade. Fed him. Took care of his knee—"

Laurel gently laid her hand on his arm. "As Foxglove says, we haven't hurt Boden."

The dwarf had been looking around the glade as Foxglove spoke. Now she turned to Laurel. "Then where is he?"

"He left when he heard you were coming," Laurel replied.

The young dwarf frowned.

Laurel went on. "So you tell me, what do you want with him? Why is he afraid of you?"

For a moment, the dwarf looked angry enough to strike out. But then a wave of sadness passed over her face. She motioned to the others, and they lowered their spears.

"I'm sorry," the dwarf leader said. "We came seeking Boden. He was once the king of my people. We feared that he might be in danger. But it's plain that he's in no danger from you. You have been his friends."

She sighed and stared ahead with worried eyes. "He isn't afraid of me," she said. "He's just the most stubborn father a

72

dwarf could ever have!"

"He's your father?" cried Laurel.

Foxglove broke in, "That means you're..."

The dwarf bowed. "I am Zandra. Daughter of Boden, and queen since he gave up the throne."

Laurel quickly introduced herself and her friends. Then she said, "If you are his daughter, I know you care about him. Even if he did cause the Jewels of Shona to be lost."

Zandra looked surprised. "He told you that?"

"Well, not exactly," said Foxglove. "He told us the tale of the lost treasure. But he didn't tell us that he was the king. Laurel's the one who figured that out."

"I see," said Zandra, nodding her head. She went on, "Of course I care about him. We all do. Why else would we be here? And only one person ever blamed him for losing the treasure. That was my father himself."

Laurel and Foxglove just looked at one another.

Zandra went on. "I thought he had put this treasure business behind him. But after he gave up the throne, things became worse. He seemed to think about the lost treasure more and more. Two months ago, he disappeared. I was sure he had come here."

"Why didn't you look for him right away?" asked Laurel.

Zandra smiled. "You know my father," she said. "So you should be able to understand. I decided to leave him alone for a while. To let him come to his senses. But he's so proud and stubborn."

"That he is," agreed Laurel.

The dwarf queen pointed toward the gray sky. "Then the rains started, and he still hadn't returned. We began to worry. So my soldiers and I came to find him."

"You're just in time," Laurel said. "I'm sure that Boden has gone back into the cave to find the treasure. But the tunnels were already starting to flood yesterday. This rain will only make things worse."

Suddenly Laurel realized that Mistletoe and Chitters were chattering at her feet. She bent down and listened carefully.

"They know exactly where your father has been working," Laurel told Zandra. "They'll lead us to him!"

"You talk to the creatures of the forest?" asked Zandra. "Another time you must tell me about this gift. But now—"

"Now we'd better get going," suggested Foxglove.

Zandra nodded. She called two of the guards to her side before turning to Laurel and the animals. "Show us the way."

A flash of lightning lit the sky, making everyone jump. It was followed by a bone-shaking thunderclap. Then, as if the lightning had cracked open the clouds, rain began to pour down.

"Quickly!" called Laurel as Mistletoe and Chitters headed for the cave entrance. "We must find Boden. Before it's too late!"

CHAPTER ELEVEN

Too Much Treasure

t was raining so hard that Laurel was almost glad to see the shelter of the cave. But once she was inside, the darkness closed in on her.

Foxglove grabbed some torches that lay near the entrance. He passed one each to Laurel, Zandra, and the two guards. Laurel lit the torches, thankful for the shaky light they cast.

"Okay, Mistletoe and Chitters," she called. "Lead us to Boden."

The animals went the same way they had gone the day before. Laurel, Foxglove, and the dwarves followed.

Water was pouring down the walls now. Puddles covered most of the tunnel floor. Laurel soon gave up trying to steer clear of them. She just waded right through, hoping none were more than knee-deep. Several times she slipped and almost fell. But each time, one of the dwarves caught her.

"How much longer?" Foxglove called out to Mistletoe.

"Not too far now," the mouse squeaked back.

Then they heard Chitters. "He's not here!"

The group hurried around the next corner. They entered the part of the tunnel where the animals had seen Boden working. The dwarf's pick and walking stick stood nearby. But there was no sign of him.

"This is where he was, Laurel!" said Mistletoe. "I'm sure of it!"

Laurel studied the small chamber. "I don't see where he could have gone," she said. "The only way out is the way we just came."

Zandra and her guards began to explore the room too. They walked along the walls, looking for signs of the old dwarf.

Then Foxglove called, "Over here!"

Laurel looked up. The pixie had climbed to the top of a rock pile.

"There's a hole!" Foxglove exclaimed. "I think he went through!" He grabbed a big rock and shoved it aside. Then he peered through the opening.

Laurel fluttered up beside Foxglove. She could see why he'd gone no farther. The opening led to a ledge. And the ledge overlooked a huge cavern.

She held on to a nearby rock and leaned out a little more. Far below, a single torch lit an unbelievable scene. Treasure lay all over the floor of the cavern. Crystal necklaces and golden bracelets. Silver goblets and jewel-covered chests. The light sparkled off of everything—everything that wasn't covered with water, that is. For at one corner, water was rushing in. And the pool at the bottom of the cavern was rising steadily.

"I see a torch. So Boden has to be there. But how did he get down?" Laurel asked.

"That's how he did it," answered Foxglove. He pointed to a rock. Laurel could see that a spike had been hammered into it. And from the spike hung a rope.

Foxglove leaned over and yelled Boden's name. By now Zandra had joined them at the top of the rock pile. She also lay on her stomach and poked her head through the opening.

"Father!" she shouted.

An answer came booming back. "Zandra! What are you doing here? Get out! And take Laurel and Foxglove with you!"

A movement below caught the eyes of the three watchers. Boden was standing in the shadows. Water already covered his feet.

"I'm not leaving without you!" Zandra called.

"Well, I'm not leaving without the Jewels of Shona!" Boden replied. "I knew I was close yesterday! I told myself then that I wouldn't lose them again!"

"Oh no!" cried Laurel. "It's our fault. If he hadn't stopped to rescue us, he might have the treasure already."

"Even if that's true, it doesn't matter," said Zandra. "Right now, we just need to get him out of there!"

The queen leaned over the edge. "Father, please come up. I don't care—"

"I do!" replied Boden. "Let me get back to work."

They watched as Boden limped around below, splashing through the rising water. Moving from one piece of treasure to the next, he stuffed each into a bag. Meanwhile, the water continued to gush down the cavern walls. The pool grew deeper, creeping like a restless snake around Boden's feet.

At last Boden put the bag over one shoulder. "I'm on my way!" he shouted to them.

The dwarf reached for the rope. But the weight of the bag threw him off balance, and he fell. Boden struggled to his feet, dripping and spluttering. He grabbed the rope again.

Zandra called down, "Let us help you!"

Boden just shook his head. Zandra sighed. "Stubborn as ever," she whispered. "I'll have to let him try to do it himself."

Laurel held her breath as Boden began his climb. At first he made steady progress. Then he began to struggle. Slower and slower he climbed. In the end, he couldn't move another inch. He simply hung there, holding on to the rope.

Zandra sat back. "Enough of this!" She called to her guards. At once the dwarves stepped out on the ledge and grabbed the rope.

"Hang on!" Zandra called down to her father. "We're going to pull you up!"

Carefully they pulled. Bit by bit, the old dwarf got closer. But there was still a long way to go before he would be safe.

"Wait!" shouted Foxglove. "The rope is going to break!"

The dwarves could see that Foxglove was right. As they had pulled, the rope had been rubbing against the rocks. Some strands were already worn through. If the rope broke, Boden would crash to the cavern floor!

"You've got to drop the bag!" Zandra ordered her father. "It's too heavy. We can't get you *and* the treasure up!"

"I'm not coming without it!" Boden shouted weakly.

"Father," said Zandra in a gentler voice. "Can't you see? You're far more important to us than any treasure. Please drop the bag."

"No!"

Laurel could wait no longer. She knew what she had to do. No one else could help Boden now. She was frightened. But her fear for the old dwarf was greater than her fear for herself.

She darted through the opening and out onto the narrow ledge with the dwarves.

"Laurel!" cried Foxglove. "What are you going to do?"

"I'm going to help him," she said calmly.

"Your wings are wet!" exclaimed Foxglove as he climbed out to stop her.

But without replying, Laurel took off. There was no time to waste.

She soon reached Boden's side and fluttered there.

"What are you doing?" asked Boden in a tired, cross voice.

"Give me the bag," said Laurel. "I'll carry it."

"Don't be foolish," Boden answered. "You'd never be able to get back up there while carrying this."

"Don't *you* be foolish," replied Laurel. "You can't climb any farther with that bag. And the rope is starting to break from the weight. Give me the bag," she repeated.

Laurel beat her wings faster in an effort to stay level with Boden. But it was growing harder by the moment. She was starting to sink toward the floor. Finally she grabbed hold of a rock that stuck out from the cave wall.

Boden stared at Laurel. And she stared steadily back at him.

The old dwarf sighed. He glanced once more at the bag in his hand. Then he held out the bag—and dropped it into the water below.

"Boden!" Laurel gasped.

"It seems that neither of us gets to play the part of hero," Boden grunted. "Now back to that ledge." He tipped his head and shouted to his daughter. "Pull!"

The guards went into action. With less weight at the end of the rope, they were able to pull Boden up.

Laurel stayed by his side, just in case the dwarf's tired hands started to slip.

They'd almost reached the ledge when it happened. One of the guards stumbled. A rock came spinning down.

Foxglove screamed a warning. "Laurel, look out!"

Laurel tried to get out of the way. But the rock hit the tip of one wing. The blow was too much for the woodfairy. She felt herself sinking.

I'm not going to make it, she thought.

CHAPTER TWELVE

A Night of Celebration

aurel heard a scrambling sound above. Boden! He'd reached the ledge. At least *he* was safe.

But Laurel was struggling to stay in the air. She knew her wings couldn't carry her to safety.

Suddenly the rope was hanging in front of her. "Grab it!" yelled Zandra.

Laurel reached for the rope. She hung on as tightly as she could and closed her eyes.

Quickly the dwarves began pulling her up. It was a race against time. Would the last strands break before they got her to the top?

But the rope held, and Laurel made it to the ledge. From there Foxglove pulled her back into the chamber.

The pixie was shaking. "Laurel! Don't you ever scare me like that again!"

Laurel smiled weakly before turning to Zandra and the guards. "Thank you," she said.

Hands on her hips, the dwarf queen frowned. "That was a foolish thing to do!" she said. Then her voice softened, and her lips curved in a smile. "Also a very brave thing. It is we who should thank you."

Next Boden stepped forward, his dark eyes gleaming. For a moment, Laurel thought he too was angry with her. But then the old dwarf bowed to her.

"You *are* brave," he whispered gruffly. "Are you sure you're not part dwarf?"

Laurel laughed. "I'm not," she said. "But you almost make me wish I were!"

"That's good enough for me," said Boden.

"I think we'd better get out of here," said Zandra. "Before this part of the cave floods too."

Boden looked longingly at the opening that led to the treasure. But Zandra put an arm around his shoulders. "Father," she said gently. "The only thing our people need returned to them is you. Forget the treasure."

Boden sighed. "Maybe we can send some miners to dig it out."

"Maybe, Father," said Zandra. "For now, let's just worry about finding dry ground."

The small band struggled back through the slippery tunnel. The water running down the walls was flowing even faster now. And the puddles on the floor had turned into a stream.

"I'm an old fool!" Laurel heard Boden mutter. "If something happens to anyone because of me…"

Laurel took the dwarf's hand in hers. "We're going to be fine," she said.

"I hope so, Laurel," said Boden. "Stubborn foolishness led to my downfall once before. Now I seem to be repeating my mistakes. And putting others in danger by doing so."

Foxglove glanced up sharply. In a whisper heard only by Laurel, he said, "You're not the only one."

For the rest of the trip, no one spoke. It took all of their energy just to make it through the tunnel.

The journey seemed endless. But at long last, they

reached the small chamber near the cave entrance.

They stopped for a moment to catch their breath. Everyone was shivering from the chilly water and the danger.

"Maybe we should wait here for a bit, Father," Zandra suggested. "At least until the rain lets up. I don't think the water will rise—"

She was interrupted by a rumbling noise that echoed through the cave. Everyone looked around to see what was happening.

Boden guessed first. "A cave-in!" he yelled. "The tunnels are giving way! Run!"

And they did. As the rumbling grew louder and louder, they ran faster. Behind them, they could hear rocks crashing from the walls.

The cave entrance came into view. Huge rocks fell at their heels as they tore out into the open air.

"Move away!" Zandra ordered the waiting soldiers. The well-trained dwarves went into action. In a minute, everyone was safely away from the cave.

They turned around to look. The rumbling from inside the cave grew to a mighty roar. It was as though they stood in the heart of a thunderstorm. Then the wave of sound reached the entrance. In seconds the cave opening was gone. A pile of rock stood in its place.

Gradually the noise stopped. In the terrible quiet that followed; Boden slowly walked toward the cave. He stared at the blocked entrance, shaking his head.

Zandra followed him. "Come, Father," she said softly. "There's time enough for making plans tomorrow. Let's rest now."

Boden nodded sadly.

The old dwarf and Zandra turned to go back to the glade. At that, the captain of the guard gave a signal. In silence the dwarf soldiers bowed to Boden. He bowed back, his eyes glowing with pride.

Zandra quietly gave some orders to her soldiers. In no time, the group was settled in a dry spot under the trees. A warm fire and hot food helped comfort them.

For the next several hours, everyone rested. Some slept, while others simply enjoyed being out of the rain.

Late that afternoon, the storm stopped. The sun peeked from behind the clouds. Before long a rainbow stretched across the valley. And a gentle breeze began to dry things out.

"It looks like the storm is over," said Foxglove. He moved out into the open, lifting his muddy face to the sun.

"Thank goodness!" said Laurel, who had followed him. She glanced down at her dress. "I'm going to wash up and change clothes," she said.

"At least you have something else to wear," said Foxglove. "I'm going to have to take a bath, tunic and all!"

Laurel found a quiet spot by the stream. She scrubbed off the cave mud. Then she changed into a fresh dress she had brought along. It felt so good to be clean—and dry!

By the time Laurel got back to the camp, everything—and everyone—looked different. Mistletoe and Chitters had cleaned their fur. Foxglove's tunic was damp, but most of the mud was gone. And the dwarves who had gone into the cave now wore dry clothing.

The glade was filled with activity. Some dwarves were

building a huge fire. Others were rolling logs into place to use as seats. Another group was fixing the evening meal.

Zandra came up to Laurel and Foxglove. "We would like to thank you for helping my father. It would be an honor if you would join us in a celebration."

Laurel smiled. "We'd love to," she said.

"Thank you," added Foxglove.

Noisy chatters and squeaks drew Zandra's eyes to Chitters and Mistletoe. She laughed. "I don't know what they're saying. But they're invited too."

Soon Laurel and Foxglove were seated by the fire. Dwarves brought them steaming bowls of soup, thick chunks of bread, and mugs of tea. Mistletoe and Chitters sat on a log, happily chewing some nuts.

After everyone had eaten, Queen Zandra stood. "Stories are part of every dwarf celebration," she said. "And now our greatest storyteller has been returned to us." She looked at Boden. "Will you tell us a tale, Father?"

Boden grunted. "A story, is it? A piece of my tired old history?" But Laurel could tell he was pleased.

The old dwarf moved closer to the fire. He sat in silence, studying his listeners. Then he began his story.

"Once upon a time, deep in the forest, there lived a wood-fairy," he began. "This fairy was a remarkable creature—with three remarkable friends. One day they all set out on a brave adventure."

Laurel glanced at Foxglove and the two animals. They could hardly believe their ears. Boden's story was going to be about them!

They leaned closer to listen. Boden spoke of the way he had roared at them when they first met. He explained how they'd fixed up his camp. And how that gift had warmed his heart. He shared the fear he'd felt while in the flooding cavern. And he told about how glad he was to be rescued.

No one made a sound as the old dwarf's story unfolded. All eyes were fixed on him as he acted out each scene. All ears followed his voice as it changed from booming shouts to faint whispers. He made everything come alive. To Laurel and her friends, it was like living through the adventure again.

When Boden was done, the dwarves leapt from their seats. They gave a great cheer for their old king.

"Another!" they cried in one voice.

But Boden refused. "Thank you for honoring me. But not tonight, my friends," he said in a tired voice.

Laurel stood. "May I tell one of Boden's stories to you?" she asked.

Zandra stared at her in surprise. "You know his stories well enough to tell them?" she asked.

Laurel reached for her bag and pulled out her journal. "I wrote the story in here," she said. She explained about her journal and how she recorded things in it. Then she opened the book. "This is the tale of the Jewels of Shona," she announced.

Laurel read straight through. She paused only once to steal a glance at Boden. The old dwarf was leaning back in his seat, his eyes fixed on the campfire.

When she finished, Laurel looked out at the dwarves. "The ending of this story was written today. When your king bravely tried to save the treasure. And when his people just as bravely saved him."

She turned to Boden. "When I record the rest of your tale, I will also record how proud I am to have met you." She

bowed to the dwarf king. Then she took her seat again.

For several moments, no one made a sound. At last Boden stood and bowed back to Laurel. Zandra and the other dwarves began to clap. Laurel ducked her head shyly.

Then Boden limped into the center of the glade. "The story still isn't complete," he announced. He reached into a pocket of his robe and pulled out a circlet of gold.

"The crown of Shona!" cried Zandra. "Father, how did you get that?"

"You didn't think I'd leave every bit of the treasure behind, did you?" said Boden. "I had this in my pocket. And I wasn't about to throw it back with the rest."

He stood in front of Zandra. "This crown belonged to Queen Shona. Every dwarf king or queen since that time has worn it. Now you will be able to wear it as well."

Boden placed the crown on his daughter's head. Then he gave her a loving hug.

Once again the dwarves cheered. And this time, Laurel and her friends joined in.

The dwarf queen signaled for silence. "I see the time has come for the giving of gifts." She turned to Laurel and Foxglove. "We have something for our new friends," she said.

"First—a gift for Laurel. A tool to use when writing in your journal," said Zandra. She handed the woodfairy a small golden box set with sparkling crystals.

"Oh, how beautiful!" exclaimed Laurel.

"It was made by my grandmother," said Zandra. "I have carried it with me since I was a child. And now I would like you to have it."

Laurel opened the box. Inside was a lovely pen made entirely of gold.

"Thank you," she breathed. "I'll treasure it always."

Zandra turned to Foxglove next. "My father tells me that you are a great scavenger," she said. "He has asked me to give you this bag. He made it from silver threads long ago."

"I was going to use it to bring out more of the treasure," explained Boden. "But I'd be honored if you would take it for a scavenging bag."

Foxglove accepted the gift. "I don't know what to say." Then he laughed and put it over one shoulder. "No pixie has ever had such a fine scavenging bag," he said. "I'll think of all of you every time I carry it."

Foxglove paused. He looked over at Laurel, who smiled and nodded her head.

With a deep sigh, Foxglove reached under his cloak and brought out his old bag. "I have something for you too," he said.

The pixie pulled out the bits of treasure he had collected. "These must have fallen into the stream and been carried down the mountain," Foxglove said. "I was going to keep them. But now that I know where they belong, I've changed my mind."

Foxglove gave the two gold chains and the red jewel to Zandra. He explained how he had found each. When he was done, the dwarves clapped once more.

The celebration continued into the night. The sky darkened and filled with stars. As sparks rose from the fire, they looked like new stars making their way home.

And still the dwarves sang and told stories. Laurel and Foxglove sang along and listened to the tales. Never before had they been part of such a wonderful gathering.

At last the celebration began to wind down. Dwarves drifted off to find places to sleep. Boden settled down in his hammock. Foxglove curled up in a blanket, his back against a log. Mistletoe and Chitters lay next to him.

Several dwarves remained by the fire, singing softly. Laurel could barely hear the words, but the tune was lovely.

She reached for her journal. Then, with her new pen, she recorded everything that had happened that day.

But that wasn't all Laurel wrote. She also told how she'd felt. She wrote of her fear in the cave. About how thankful she'd been when she and Boden were saved. She told of her pride in helping the old dwarf. And she wrote about the excitement of the celebration and the joy of making new friends.

Finally Laurel closed her journal. She placed the pen carefully in its box. But she didn't feel ready for sleep. The day had been too full. Too wonderful and marvelous. She didn't want it to end just yet.

With a contented sigh, Laurel leaned back and listened to the dwarves' gentle singing.

CHAPTER THIRTEEN

Sharing Treasures

e're almost home," said Laurel happily. She and her friends had been walking through the Great Forest most of the day. After the darkness of the Deeps, the forest didn't seem so frightening.

"Home! Home! Home!" cried Chitters.

"I can't wait," added Mistletoe.

Laurel turned to Foxglove. "Why don't you come and have something to eat?" she asked.

"A wonderful idea," said Foxglove.

Laurel and her friends had left Boden's glade the day before. The dwarves had walked with them to the base of the mountain. There they had parted with promises to visit one another.

"I hope we do get to visit the dwarves someday," said Laurel thoughtfully.

"That would be a real adventure," agreed Foxglove. "No other pixie has ever been asked to do that!"

"Can we go along?" asked Chitters.

"Of course," said Laurel. "We'd never leave you two behind."

They reached the edge of the Dappled Woods. Laurel looked around with a smile. A soft breeze chased through the trees. Butterflies flitted from blossom to blossom. In the branches overhead, birds sang sweet tunes.

How beautiful it is here! And how safe. Adventuring is fine, thought Laurel. But coming home was even better.

Before long they heard the roar of Thunder Falls. And soon they could see the waterfall. They worked their way down the rocky slope to the pond below.

"We made it!" sighed Laurel. "Now let's go up to my treehouse and fix something to eat."

She looked at the animals. "Are you coming?" she asked.

"No," said Mistletoe. "I've had all the up and down I want for a while."

"Me too!" added Chitters.

While the two animals raced off, Laurel and Foxglove climbed the ladder to the treehouse.

Laurel was happy to see that everything looked just as she'd left it. She sighed and dropped her traveling bag on her bed. Then she fixed a snack and took it out to the porch.

The friends ate in comfortable silence. They were just finishing their meal when they heard a voice below.

"Laurel! Foxglove!"

"Ivy!" said Laurel, jumping to her feet. She stepped off her porch and glided to the ground. Foxglove climbed down the ladder.

Ivy threw her arms around Laurel. "Oh, I'm so glad to see you! I was beginning to worry. But when I saw Mistletoe and Chitters, I knew you were back."

"Wait until you hear what we've been doing," said Foxglove.

"Did you find the lost treasure?" asked Ivy.

Laurel and Foxglove stared at one another. Then they broke into laughter.

"Well," said Laurel. "We *saw* the treasure. But I wouldn't say we exactly *found* it!"

"However, we did find a lost king!" added Foxglove.

Ivy grinned. "I want to hear everything! We all do. I'm supposed to take you right to the clearing."

"You go ahead, Laurel," said Foxglove. "I'm going home now. Thanks to you—and Boden—I've got a wonderful story to tell too. And a brand-new scavenging bag to show off."

With a wave, the pixie headed off. As they walked toward the clearing, Laurel and Ivy could hear his happy whistle.

When they arrived, many fairies were already waiting. Everyone wanted to know what Laurel had been up to this time. Like Ivy, the other fairies had no wish to leave their woods. But they enjoyed the wonderful stories that Laurel always brought back with her.

Laurel greeted her friends and teachers. Questions came at her from all sides, and she did her best to answer them. Only Primrose stood off by herself. As usual she tried to act as if she wasn't interested. But she actually hung on every word.

The Eldest joined the group late. She nodded to Laurel. "Home from another adventure in the Great Forest, I see."

"Yes," Laurel replied. "And I recorded everything in my journal. My own story and that of the old dwarf king!"

The Eldest laughed. "It sounds wonderfully exciting," she said. "And we'd love to hear what you wrote in your journal."

Everyone settled down on the soft grass that carpeted the glade. Complete silence fell over the group.

Laurel picked up her journal and started to read.

Today company came calling...

Laurel read every word she had written about her latest

adventures. She told of the wonders she'd seen, the friends she'd made, and the lessons she'd learned. Her listeners laughed, gasped, and cheered in all the right places.

Finally Laurel reached the last bit of her story.

> I used to be afraid of dark, closed-in spaces. I still am! But now I know I can make my way past my fears. And do what needs to be done.

She smiled and closed her journal. How happy she was to be able to share this part of her history. And how glad she was that she'd written it all down. Years from now, others could read about it too.

The Eldest stood. "That was fine work, Laurel. You made everything seem so real."

Laurel smiled. "Thank you," she said. And she said a silent thank-you to Boden as well. The old dwarf had shown her how to make her journal come alive.

Then Laurel remembered one more thing she wanted to do. She reached into her cloak and pulled out the golden box. "I almost forgot!" she said. "Here's the pen Queen Zandra gave me. It's a piece of dwarf treasure for all woodfairies."

Laurel opened the box. The other woodfairies gathered around her, exclaiming at the sight.

"It's beautiful, Laurel," said the Eldest. "But what did you mean when you said it was a treasure for all woodfairies?"

Laurel laughed. "Well, you probably know that I tend to lose things."

A number of smiles told Laurel that many of her fairy friends did know this.

She went on. "Since this is so special, I don't want anything to happen to it. I thought...I mean, I wondered..." She stopped and looked up at the Eldest. "I thought we might keep it here in the Ancient Clearing. And use it when we write in the Chronicles."

The old fairy looked surprised. Then she smiled warmly at Laurel. "I think that's a fine idea," she said. "And it will do honor to the dwarves' wonderful gift."

Laurel handed the box to the Eldest. The old fairy carried it to the stump where the book of Chronicles was kept. She opened the stump, then paused and turned to Laurel.

"I think you should do this," the Eldest suggested.

So Laurel held the golden box one more time. Gently she placed it inside the stump. The Eldest closed the door.

Laurel stood quietly in front of the tree stump. She felt a strange mix of wonder and pride. Now two treasures rested inside, one from the woodfairies and the other from the dwarves. Both were—and always would be—parts of their shared histories.

More to Explore

Have fun exploring more about the wonderful treasures of the forest. And there are great projects for you to do too!

A Journal of Your Own

You can keep a journal, just like Laurel does. And like Laurel, you can make your own journal. Simply follow the directions below.

What you need

- Two pieces of heavy cardboard
- Sharp scissors
- Cover material (wallpaper scraps, gift wrap, shelf paper, or paper you've decorated yourself)
- Clear-drying glue
- ½"-wide clear tape
- Awl or large nail
- Ruler
- Pencil
- Hole punch
- 20 to 30 sheets of paper (lined or unlined)
- One yard thin ribbon or heavy yarn

What you do

1. Decide how large you want your journal to be. Cut two pieces of cardboard to that size.

2. Choose your cover material from the list of suggestions. Cut two pieces. Each should be about twice as large as the cardboard.

3. Apply a thin layer of glue to the top side of one cardboard cover. Wet your fingers and smooth the glue over the cardboard, all the way to the edges. Wash and dry your hands.

4. Place one piece of cover material on a flat surface, good side down. Place the cardboard cover in the center of the cover material, glue side down. Press down on all sides. Allow the glue to dry. Repeat steps 3 and 4 for the second cover.

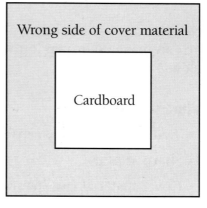

Wrong side of cover material

Cardboard

Step 4

5. Apply glue to the back side of the cardboard. Then wrap the extra cover material around to the back, as if you were gift-wrapping a package. Add glue as needed to hold the edges down. If necessary, use a little tape to hold the corners. Repeat the steps for the second cover. Allow the glue to dry.

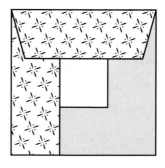

Step 5

6. Cut another piece of cover material just a little smaller than the cover itself. Spread a thin layer of glue over the inside back of the cover. Then place the piece of cover material over the back side. Repeat the steps for the second cover. Allow the glue to dry.

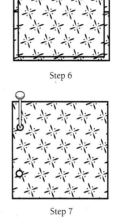

Step 6

7. With an awl or large nail, punch two holes along one side of the front cover. Holes should be ½" to ¾" from the outside edge. Punch matching holes in the back cover.

Step 7

8. With a ruler, draw a line on the inside of the covers, about 1" from the edge with holes.

9. Place the ruler on the line and hold it down firmly. Bend the cover along the line you drew. Then turn the cover over and bend in the other direction. Repeat the steps with the back cover.

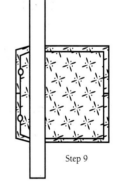

10. Cut the paper for your journal pages. Pages should be about ¼" smaller than the covers on all sides.

Step 9

11. Place the front cover on top of one journal page, in about ¼" from the edge. Mark where the holes should be. With the hole punch, make holes in each journal page.

12. Place the journal pages between the covers, lining up all holes. Cut the ribbon or yarn into two pieces. String through the holes and tie in a pretty bow.

Nature Scavenger Hunt

Are you a good observer of nature? Find out by going on a nature scavenger hunt.

First copy the list below onto a sheet of paper. Then head outside. You can hunt in your backyard, at a nearby park, or in any other outdoor area.

How many of the things on the list can you spot? Don't worry if you can't find them all. Just check off the ones that you do see. Then count them up. Try to find at least ten things. You might also choose to race against the clock by setting yourself a time limit.

Look for

- pinecone
- smooth rock
- V-shaped twig
- tree shorter than you are
- bird with some red on it
- flying insect
- spiderweb
- creature that lives under a rock
- tree with rough bark
- animal track

- butterfly or moth
- animal with fur
- nut in its shell
- wild mushroom
- moss
- evergreen branch
- tree or bush with berries
- natural body of water
- puffy white cloud
- insect smaller than your fingernail

Woodland Art

Try these art projects with common woodland materials. Like Laurel, you can use these ideas to decorate your bedroom. They also make great gifts for someone special.

Dried flower bouquets

You can save pretty flowers and leaves by drying them. When plants dry, they usually change. They may shrink and turn brown. But they will still look and smell interesting.

Collect flowers and leaves on a sunny morning. Be sure they are dry when you pick them. And leave a fairly long stem on each plant.

Arrange four or five plants into a small bouquet. Tie the stems together with string. Then hang them upside down in a dark, dry spot.

Check every day. When your plants are completely dry, take them down. Display the bouquet in a small vase.

Pressed flower artwork

Another way to save plants is to press them. Choose flowers that don't have a thick middle section. Violets, delphinium, lily of the valley, pansies, cornflowers, and small daisies are all good choices.

Place a layer of newspaper on a flat surface. Put several paper towels on top of the newspaper. Then arrange flowers and cover them with another layer of paper towels. Stack two or three heavy books on top of the pile.

Check your flowers in three or four days. They should be dry and flat. Carefully remove them from the paper towel. Then use the flowers to decorate bookmarks or notepaper. Or make an arrangement on paper and frame it as a work of art.

Sun prints

Let the sun do the work for this project! Pick several interesting leaves. Arrange them on black or dark blue construction paper. You may want to use small rolls of cellophane tape to hold the leaves in place. Be sure the tape is under the leaf and can't be seen.

Find a sunny indoor spot to place the colored paper. Leave the paper there for several days. Then carefully remove the leaves. The sunlight should have caused the paper that wasn't covered to fade. But where the leaves hid the paper, you'll still have the original color—and a print of each leaf's shape!

Woodfairy Feast

Have a woodfairy feast. Make some delicious fairy cakes to serve. Then choose some special touches from the suggestions found on page 104. Be sure to invite a friend or two to share the feast.

Fairy cakes

It's easy to make Fairy Cakes if you use packaged mixes. Be sure you get permission to use the oven, or ask an adult for help.

Fairy Cakes

What you need
Packaged cake or cupcake mix
Frosting mix or ready-made frosting
Sprinkles, small candies, or decorator frosting

What you do
1. Follow the package directions to prepare the cake mix.
2. Line a cupcake pan with cupcake papers. (If possible, use a miniature cupcake pan and papers so you can

Fairy Cakes (cont'd)

make fairy-sized cakes.)
3. Fill each cup about 3/4 of the way with cake mix.
4. Bake at the temperature indicated on the package. (If there are no directions for miniature cupcakes, subtract ten minutes from the time given for regular cupcakes. Just to be sure, check the cupcakes before the time is up.)
5. When the cupcakes are cool, frost them.
6. Decorate the tops with sprinkles, candies, or decorator frosting.

Special touches

Try some of these ideas to make your fairy feast an event that's extra special.

- Decorate your table with small vases of real or artificial flowers.

- Woven place mats and napkins will help create a fairy-like scene. Add pretty glasses or teacups, small plates (doll dishes will work), and silverware.

- Trace the pattern below to make small leaf-shaped doilies from colored paper. Place one or more paper leaves on each plate. Then set a cupcake on top.

- Fill a pitcher with something to drink. Lemonade, fruit juice, or tea with honey are all things Laurel might serve.

- You may want to add a few of these treats to your table: green mints, fruit slices, or berries.

Stardust Story Sampler

Stardust Classics books feature other heroines to believe in. Come explore with Kat the Time Explorer and Alissa, Princess of Arcadia. Here are short selections from their books.

Selection from

KAT AND THE EMPEROR'S GIFT

"I wonder where we ended up this time," said Kat as she brushed snow from her cheeks.

"And when," added Jessie with a smile. She led the way down the alley. In the bitter cold, the snow beneath their feet crunched like broken glass.

The alley came to an end at a stone-paved street. Kat and Jessie stepped out and looked around. The street stretched out wide and straight in a seemingly endless line. Along both sides of the roadway stood sturdy wooden buildings. And there were people everywhere.

To their left, a door opened, and a blast of warm air flowed out. With it came the sound of a cheerful voice.

"I will have some more fine silks next week. The finest in all of Ta-tu! Be sure to come back."

A man carrying a package hurried out the door. He gave Jessie and Kat a curious look before heading off.

"These buildings must be shops," said Kat.

"Let's go inside," suggested Jessie. "Maybe we can find out where we are."

They rang the bell. At once a short, smiling man opened the door. For a moment, he looked startled. Then he bowed and motioned them inside. "Come in! Come in! Step out of the cold!"

Kat and Jessie happily entered the warmth of the shop. They stopped and stared in delight as they took in the richness around them. Rolls of lovely fabric rose in stacks almost to the ceiling.

In a far corner, a tall man stood with his back to them. He thoughtfully stroked a bolt of red silk.

The merchant studied Kat and Jessie. "You must be visitors," he said. "Welcome to Ta-tu."

Kat nodded and Jessie answered quietly, "Thank you."

At the sound of Jessie's voice, the other customer turned and looked at them. "You are Europeans!" he exclaimed. His bearded face broke into a huge smile, and he hurried across the room.

Kat and Jessie smiled in response. The speaker was obviously a European—the first they'd seen.

"This is truly amazing," the man continued. "I had thought my father, my uncle, and I were the only Europeans in these parts. But here you are! And women as well! May I ask what brings you here?"

Jessie and Kat felt tongue-tied. What could they say? They didn't even know where "here" was yet.

Fortunately the stranger was so excited that he provided them with an answer. "You must be fellow explorers!" He glanced around. "But where is the rest of your party?"

"Party?" echoed Kat weakly.

"We're not with any party," added Jessie.

"What!" exclaimed the man with surprise. "You came all the way alone? Surely not on such a long and dangerous trip!"

When Kat and Jessie didn't respond, the man gave them a

knowing look. "Ah," he said. "I have seen this happen before to travelers. My guess is that your guides turned out to be thieves. How terrible! But where are you staying here in Ta-tu?"

"We don't have a place to stay," said Jessie.

"And did the thieves take all your belongings?" he asked.

"We have nothing except these two bags," answered Kat.

"Two bags!" repeated the man. "Let me set your worries to rest. I shall take care of things for you." With a bow, he added, "My name is Marco Polo. And I am at your service."

Selection from

ALISSA AND THE CASTLE GHOST

Balin closed his book and handed it to Princess Alissa.

"I've marked a spell for you to practice," the wizard said. "And now you'd better be going. Didn't you come here early this afternoon because you have to meet with Sir Drear?"

That's right," said Alissa. "Lia and I are having a history lesson in the portrait gallery."

"Well, off with you then," said the wizard. "And keep an open mind, Alissa. You may actually learn something interesting from Sir Drear."

"I doubt it," said Alissa. "But I'll try."

The princess pulled open the door and headed down the twisting steps. Before long she had crossed the courtyard and entered the castle.

"There you are!" said Lia. "I was afraid you'd be late. And you know that makes Sir Drear cross."

"Sir Drear is always cross," said Alissa. "Do you think all stewards are like that?"

Lia laughed. "Well, running a kingdom is hard work. But I think he may be crabbier than most."

Lia got up from the bench where she'd been waiting. Together the girls walked through the arched doorway that led to the portrait gallery.

Lia walked slowly through the gallery, studying the portraits. But Alissa stopped at a window. She gazed longingly at the sunlit gardens below.

"I don't see why Sir Drear needs to show us the portraits," she said. "I've been coming here since I was small. It's not like anything ever changes. Just walls filled with paintings of people dead long ago. Every one of them sad and gloomy too."

"Maybe you haven't been looking carefully then," said Lia. "Because *he* certainly isn't sad or gloomy."

Alissa quickly joined Lia. Her friend was standing in front of a portrait of an elderly man. He was gray-haired and gray-eyed. His lips were turned up in a warm smile. And there was a friendly gleam in his eyes.

"I've never seen this portrait before!" said Alissa in surprise. She checked the nameplate on the wooden frame.

" 'Sir Grendon,' " she read. "I haven't heard of him either. And he looks like someone I'd want to know."

At the sound of footsteps, both girls moved away from the portrait. Sir Drear had arrived. Alissa and Lia watched as the tall, bony steward approached. His head was down, and he was reading some papers he had in his hands.

Alissa sighed. It was time to listen to Drear go on and on

about the kingdom's history. He especially liked to talk about his own ancestors. Drear felt that every one of them had played an important part in Arcadia's past.

When he reached the girls, Sir Drear looked up. As usual, his thin lips formed a straight line across his gray face.

But instead of beginning the lesson, the steward dropped his papers. A shocked look washed over his face. Then two large spots of red appeared on his cheeks.

Slowly Drear raised a shaking hand and pointed toward Alissa. In a loud voice he cried, "What is the meaning of that?"

STARDUST CLASSICS titles are written under pseudonyms. Authors work closely with Margaret Hall, executive editor of Just Pretend.

Ms. Hall has devoted her professional career to working with and for children. She has a B.S. and an M.S. in education from the State University of New York at Geneseo. For many years, she taught as a classroom and remedial reading teacher for students from preschool through upper elementary. Ms. Hall has also served as an editor with an educational publisher and as a consultant for the Iowa State Department of Education. She has a long history as a freelance writer for the school market, authoring several children's books as well as numerous teacher resources.

JOEL SPECTOR, illustrator of *Laurel and the Lost Treasure,* was born in Cuba and moved to Queens, New York, when he was 12 years old. He graduated from the Fashion Institute of Technology in New York City and began his art career as a fashion illustrator.

Mr. Spector has illustrated many books and other materials. He provided illustrations for a Japanese series based on the Anne of Green Gables books. The series was intended for use in teaching English in Japan—where Anne is an extremely popular character.

Joel Spector lives in Connecticut with his wife and their four children. His eldest son, Max, was the model for Laurel's friend Foxglove.

PATRICK FARICY, the cover illustrator, was born and raised in Minnesota. He began his art education there, studying communication design, illustration, and fine art at the School of Associated Arts in St. Paul. He completed his studies at the Art Center College of Design in Pasadena, California.

Since graduating in 1991, Mr. Faricy has been living in California and working as a freelance illustrator. His clients include Coca-Cola, Kellogg's, Busch Gardens, and Warner Brothers.

When he's not painting, Patrick Faricy spends his time writing and playing music, going to the movies, and talking with friends. And he is always on the lookout for something new and different to add to his frog collection!